From the Ash She Rises

The Dreamscape Chronicles Book 1

Courtney Daybell

D1091396

FROM THE ASH SHE RISES

Copyright © 2020 by Courtney Daybell

All rights reserved.

"And just as the Phoenix rose from the ashes, she too will rise. Returning from the flames, clothed in nothing but her strength, more beautiful than ever before."
– Shannen Heartzs

Contents

Chapter 1

Cora lay buried under a cocoon of soft blankets in her room. Life had changed in ways Cora couldn't have anticipated after her brother died. The death of a young person is always unexpected, but Max's death blindsided her. It swept over Cora and her family like a tidal wave, leaving four lives bobbing in the wreckage.

Cora and Max had always been close, even though four years separated them. He hadn't laughed at her or mocked her the way their older sister did.

She'd known she would be sad. But she thought life would return back to normal, minus Max. She understood that she would always miss him, but at eleven years old, it was impossible for her to grasp how the grief would completely alter her whole family, her whole world.

It had been months since that day, and Cora was beginning to realize that maybe things would *never* be normal. Or what normal used to be. Reagan was Cora's cool older sister, and she spent every day holed up in her room, venturing out only a few times. Her mom, Julie, and her dad, Ned, tried their best to resume life as it used to be, but sometimes when Cora saw them, they reminded her of ghosts, floating through the house with vacant, glazed eyes.

Cora's room still had the semblances of her childhood. Her cherished stuffed dolphin was shoved haphazardly at the end of her bed. She was too old to actually admit sleeping with a stuffed animal, but she wasn't quite old enough to banish it completely. Her canopy bed was draped with feather-light, ethereal tulle. The room was swathed in pale pinks with accents of gold adding a touch of glamor. It was a room fit for the five-year-old princess she'd once been. She had grown out of it somewhere along the way, but the decor hadn't changed.

Cora had added new elements to her room, reflective of her emerging pre-teen self. Penciled sketches hung from every open spot of wall; framed photos of Cora and her best friend Mia graced the shelves. Not only was Mia Cora's best friend, but she was really her only friend. Mia had moved into the neighborhood when the girls were in third grade, and they'd been inseparable ever since. They saw each other almost every day, at school or meeting to ride bikes.

Cora rolled onto her back and caught sight of the woven wall hanging positioned above her bed. Crystals hung from the woven fabric, dotting the web like brightly colored spiders. Fresh tears pricked her eyes as a flood of memories of Max overcame her. The wall hanging was a souvenir she'd picked up on a family trip in Sedona the summer before. She remembered how the crystals had caught her eye, luring her in like a magnet. A single bright blue stone, blue apatite, beacon. Reagan had rolled her eyes and scoffed.

"That's lame," Reagan had said under her breath. Quiet enough that Cora's parents couldn't hear. "Fitting for Cora." She sneered.

Max had defended her choice. "Don't listen to her. This thing is cool," he said, inspecting each crystal, lingering on the vibrant blue apatite.

A pang of loneliness pricked her heart at the memory, like the sting of a rubber band on her skin, but she let herself sit in the memory, absorbing everything she could, wallowing in remembrance of Max. He'd bought something at the store that day, too. Max had picked a small gold compass as his souvenir, the size of a quarter and a dull, faded gold. Worn with time and age.

There was a knock at the door and Cora snapped back to reality, leaving Max's memory in Sedona. Her mom's head poked through a crack in the door. Her mom, normally coiffed and well-styled, looked worn down. Her short, blond hair was tied back in a tiny ponytail, a stub of hair poking from the hair elastic. Her blue eyes were bloodshot and swollen and her fair skin was especially pale, marked with red blotches that Cora assumed was from crying.

"Mia is downstairs, honey." She smiled. "Do you want to see her?"

She didn't, really. But she wanted to stay alone in her room even less. She threw back the covers and peeled herself from the bed. At the door, her mom caught her in a tight hug that made Cora want to break.

Mia stood at the counter, but turned when she heard Cora's feet coming down the stairs. She looked down a little when she saw Cora's red-rimmed eyes. By now, Cora was used to people's discomfort around her. Most people at school didn't know what to do with Cora's tears and sadness. They mostly ignored her, while teachers pursed their lips and offered tight smiles, unsure of what to say. Mia concealed any sign of discomfort quickly, and recovered with a cheerful, "Hey!" She gave Cora a quick hug.

"Hey." Cora returned the embrace awkwardly. Suddenly, the need to get out of the house was overwhelming. She knew Mia would have ridden her bike over. "Want to go on a bike ride?"

Mia nodded, and they looked at Cora's mom expectantly. She nodded slightly. "Be safe, you two. And Cora," she added, "just about an hour, okay?"

"Let me just grab my shoes," Cora said, and turned to head up the stairs. She picked up her favorite shoes, a well-worn pair of pink high-top sneakers with white soles. She bounded down the stairs, stopping at the coat closet to pull out her favorite hoodie. She threw it over her shoulders, zipping it quickly and then heading out the front door with Mia.

They took off on their bikes, pedaling quickly. They raced through the neighborhood before taking a right-hand turn and pedaling up a hill. The resistance underneath her feet increased with the incline and Cora pushed to keep up her pace. Mia was right in front of her. Mia stopped and hopped off her bike.

"Hold on," Mia said, kneeling to inspect the bike chain. "My chain is messed up."

Cora dismounted her bike and sat on a bench overlooking the city as Mia fixed her bike. It was almost evening, but there was no sunset as a cloud cover obscured the sun's rays. Cora looked out at the city before them. In the distance, all the way across town, Cora noticed a building. In the top right corner of the building a window glowed with a greenish, yellow-gold glow. Cora couldn't take her eyes off of it.

Mia tinkered with her chain behind Cora. If they hurried, they could make it across town and back before Cora needed to be home. Mia finished with her chain, and

Cora balanced herself on her bike, pushing down with one foot to accelerate.

"Ready?" she asked Mia. Mia nodded.

"Follow me!" she shouted to Mia. The glow of the window was calling her, enticing her. Cora pedaled furiously, her breath quickening and her pulse racing. She wasn't an athlete and she'd never excelled at any sport, so the exertion winded her. But she kept going. Reagan was a soccer star. Colleges around the nation were vying for her to play for their elite teams, constantly sending letters and scouts to Reagan's games. And Max had been athletic in every way imaginable. Her family had joked if a ball was involved, Max was—or would be—good at it. He'd played football, basketball, baseball.

It seemed natural for Cora to follow in their footsteps, but nothing stuck. She tried soccer, and found herself counting the daffodils instead of engaging in the game. She tried basketball and softball with similar outcomes. She tried swimming, but being in a swimsuit with so much of her body exposed made her uncomfortable. So, she resigned herself to the fact that maybe she was just the only non-athletic person in the entire Jones family.

A chilly wind rustled through her hair and brought Cora back to reality as they sped toward the light.

The girls pedaled on, streaking through the roads of the city. Mia caught up to her. "Where are we even going?" she asked breathlessly, looking around for some clue to their destination.

Cora didn't know how to explain, which seemed common for her these days. She didn't know how to explain where they were going to her best friend. She didn't know how to explain how she was feeling to her parents, or anyone else who asked. It wasn't just that she didn't have adequate words, but rather, she just didn't know how she was feeling. It was as if her emotions were tangled together, impossible to tell where one ended and another began. Anger, sadness, and confusion all blended together in one jumbled mess.

"Just a little farther," Cora said. She was breathing heavily.

Cora kept her eyes trained on the glimmering building in front of her. As they approached, her heart deflated when she realized the iridescent glow had faded, leaving a dull, lackluster brick structure with dark, dim windows. She craned her neck to top corner, to the window that had sparkled with such hope. In front of her, was just a decrepit, abandoned warehouse.

"Cora?" Mia asked. She pulled up beside Cora and looked at her warmly, but quizzically. "What are we doing here?"

Cora fought back the tears that stung to her eyes and shook her head. "I thought... I thought..." She started to explain, but didn't know how. *I thought my dead brother was trying to tell me something. I thought maybe this sparkly window was him calling me.* Kids at school already gawked at her. She shook her head and let the silence hang between them, thick and awkward.

Mia looked at her, her mouth slightly open. "We should probably turn back around. I need to be home for dinner soon."

"Yeah, for sure," Cora agreed, her eyes trained on the ground in front of her, avoiding Mia's gaze. She was sweating from the exertion. She pulled off her sweatshirt and tied it around her waist. As she turned her bike around, a glimmer gold caught her eye. She wheeled over to it and hunched down. In plain sight, there lay a dull, quarter-sized gold compass.

Cora's breath caught in her chest, a gasp escaping her mouth. The compass was an exact replica of the compass Max had picked from the trading post the summer before. On the pavement, in front of this building that had called to her. Cora's heart started to race and she looked around, almost sure she would see Max's face or some other sign of him.

"Cora?" Mia called to her again. "You okay?" Mia's brow was furrowed in concern, a frown on her lips.

Cora scooped up the compass, slipped it in her pocket, and pushed the pedal down with her foot, propelling her forward. "Yeah," she said. "Just found a lucky penny."

Riding home, Cora couldn't think of anything but the compass. She and Mia made casual conversation as they rode, Cora forcing a casual-ness that betrayed her. She debated telling Mia, but the look on Mia's face from earlier haunted her, and she decided to keep the compass to herself. Mia might think she was crazy. Was she actually crazy? Maybe that wasn't Max's compass. It couldn't be... could it? It must just be one that looked like it. Since they were riding, she couldn't take it out and inspect it.

Cora knew how she could tell if it was Max's. Max had dropped it minutes after he'd bought it. It had landed squarely on a small rock, the impact leaving a circular imprint on the back. She remembered Max holding the compass between his thumb and fingers, the edge of his middle finger rubbing the indent. Did the compass from the sidewalk have that mark? She couldn't remember. Mia rode slightly ahead of her, talking about school and who liked whom and what music she was listening to. Cora listened, occasionally contributing an "Uh-huh" or "Yeah, totally." But her mind was focused solely on the compass in her pocket.

Before she realized it, they were home. They stopped in front of her coral stucco house with a palm tree planted in the yard. One year, the Jones family had opted for the tropical tree instead of a traditional Christmas tree, and when Christmas was over, they transplanted the palm in the front yard. Cora loved it. She loved the way the branches splayed out against the sky, resembling a crown of feathered leaves.

Cora looked at the front door, willing herself to go in. It wasn't the same without Max. The dynamic was different, the smell was different. The conversations were different, and Cora could tell it would be like that for a long time, maybe forever. Tears pricked in her eyes at the thought of facing the rest of her life without her beloved brother. It was too much to bear.

"Cora?" Mia called.

"Sorry," Cora apologized, and looked at Mia. "I was just kind of lost in my thoughts."

Mia nodded. "No problem. I gotta go, though. See you tomorrow!" Mia turned, pushed her weight onto one pedal, and began to glide away. Before she turned the corner, Mia gave a small wave over her shoulder. Cora raised her hand in a half-hearted wave. A twinge of envy coursed through her body. She wanted her heart to be light again.

Chapter 2

MIA PEDALED AWAY, WAVING over her shoulder. Cora waved back, and Mia couldn't help but notice that the half smile from Cora's lips never reached her eyes. Cora's eyes used to shine. They lit up, sparkled even, especially when she talked about her favorite things, like her art.

Mia didn't know what to do or how to help her friend. It was as if Cora was slowly slipping away, like a sketch that was slowly being erased. The details, the things that made the sketch come alive were slowly dissolving, with only the faintest pencil lines still visible.

She couldn't understand what Cora was going through. Mia had two siblings as well, and the thought of losing one of them made her stomach queasy and twist in knots. She shook her head, as if shaking away some terrible fate. She couldn't imagine how awful it would be to lose one of them.

Within minutes, Mia was home. As she came up the driveway, she spotted her mom, kneeling and pulling weeds from their garden bed. Her mom paused as Mia approached.

"Hey, sweetie," she said, peeling off her gardening gloves and taking Mia's hand in hers. Her hands were smooth. "How was the bike ride?"

Mia shrugged and sat down next to her mom. Seated, Mia noticed the sole of her shoe was tearing. She played with the frayed edge. "Cora's sad," she said softly, remembering her friend's solemn expression nearly the entire bike ride. "And it makes me sad. I just don't know how to help."

Her mom nodded slowly. "Cora has experienced something terrible," she said finally. "Something no one should ever have to go through. It'll take a while for her to feel like herself again, and she will probably change, too. Be patient with her. The best thing you can do is be there for her."

When Mia looked up, she saw her mother's eyes had filled with tears, the deep brown looking even richer.

"What if we thought of some things Cora loved, her favorite candy, her favorite activities, that sort of thing?" her mother asked, glancing at her watch. "If we hurry, we can run to the store and pick up a few things before dad has dinner ready."

Mia nodded.

"Let me grab the keys. I'll meet you at the car."

Mia's mom stood, brushed the lingering dirt from her pants and gloves, and gave Mia a quick kiss on the head. Minutes later, they were driving to the store, where Mia picked up some of Cora's favorite things: a sketching pencil, sour gummy candies, and a new sketch pad. If there was one thing that could make Cora's blue eyes sparkle again, it was art.

Chapter 3

CORA PUSHED THE DOOR open, greeted by a familiar smell. She instantly knew what they were having for dinner. Cora was certain it was a Jones concoction, because whenever anyone else talked about their favorite meal, it was never *her* favorite. Other kids liked spaghetti, pizza, or tacos. But no one ever said, Zippy Beans and Rice. They gave her a quizzical stare, and every time that happened, Cora resolved to come up with a safer response to avoid strange looks.

She followed the aroma to the kitchen where her mom stood, her back to Cora, stirring the rice mixture. Rice mixed with black beans, diced tomatoes, roasted peppers. Some spices and seasoning, and chicken. On special occasions, homemade tortillas and shredded cheese. Cora could see little mounds of dough for homemade tortillas, waiting to be shaped and heated on the griddle. For reasons she didn't quite understand, this sweet act of love from her mom—cooking Cora's favorite meal—made her heart ache.

Her mom must have sensed Cora's presence, because she turned around, a smile forming at her lips. "Hi, honey. How was the bike ride?"

"It was good," she said, willing herself to portray an air of nonchalance, but her hand twitched instinctively to her pocket where the compass sat, waiting.

"Dinner's almost ready," her mom said, still stirring the mixture.

"Okay." She patted her pocket. She had to see the compass. "I'll be down in a little bit," she said, turning and heading for the stairs.

"I made your zippy beans!" Her mom called after her, a plea for normalcy in her voice.

Her mom was just like that. She was the kind of mom the other kids were envious of. She bought their favorite treats and kept the pantry stocked. She was keenly aware of her kids, and Cora loved her so much for that.

Cora knew she should go down into the kitchen, help her mom, or at the very least sit and talk with her. But she had to examine the compass.

Cora sat under the canopy of her bed, her heart pounding as if it would burst through her chest. She reached into her pocket, wrapping her fingers around the compass, feeling the heat against her palm. She pulled it slowly out of her pocket and held it between her thumb and forefinger, inspecting the gilded globe. She spun the compass in her fingers, and there, on the backside of the compass she saw it. The rough imprint. She gasped. The impression was the same.

This was Max's compass. But how?

There is a logical explanation for this, her head warned.

But what? her heart countered. The odds of Max's compass being found on the other side of town—a part of town that Cora had been particularly called to—seemed unlikely. But she also knew there *had* to be a logical explanation. Right?

"Cora?" Her mom called from downstairs. "Dinner is ready!"

As she held Max's beloved compass, food was the last thing on her mind, even if it was her favorite food. But she knew dinner was the time her mom tried her hardest to make things as normal as possible. She pictured her mom down there, sitting at the table by herself as her family isolated, and couldn't stand the thought of making her mom sadder. Instead, she wistfully pocketed the compass and walked down the stairs and into the kitchen, where her mom was placing plates on the table.

"Hey sweetie," she smiled, but her eyes were rimmed with red and pink splotches splayed across her cheeks. "There's something on the counter for you."

She motioned with her head toward the kitchen table. Gossamer thin, white tissue paper with turquoise polka dots peeked from a cheery, yellow gift bag. Cora pulled a corner of the tissue paper and peered inside. A sketchpad, pencil, and a bag of Cora's favorite candy lay inside. She skimmed the card, noting Mia's meticulous writing.

Guilt gnawed at her chest for keeping the compass secret from her best friend. But she couldn't put words to what was happening, even to herself.

Julie looked over Cora's shoulder at the sketchpad and candy. "That was nice of her," she said, putting her hand on Cora's shoulder.

Cora nodded, and suddenly the weight of all the things rested on Cora's shoulders. Tears sprang to her eyes, but Cora brushed them away before her mom could see.

"I'm going to go put this in my room," she said, making the excuse to escape for a few minutes.

"Okay," Julie said, stepping aside so Cora could get by. "Come right back down for dinner, okay?" She ran her hand over Cora's hair, still reaching as Cora walked away.

Chapter 4

THE DINNER HOUR WAS one of Cora's least favorite times. What used to be a highlight of her day had turned into something she dreaded.

"Cora-bear!" her dad exclaimed, breaking the tense silence. "How was your day?" he asked, pulling out a chair and sitting at the table.

"Good," she said. She shoveled a forkful of rice and beans into her mouth, anxious to get back up to her room.

"Yeah? What was the best part so far?" He asked the same questions every night. Like the dinner hour, Cora had once loved the tradition. She loved hearing her family recount their days, ruminating on the highlights. Now, she dreaded the question. It was just one more opportunity for her to remember how much her life had changed, how much was missing without Max.

Cora was glad her mouth was full of food. The chewing gave her time to come up with an answer.

"Probably my bike ride with Mia," she answered, finally.

"That does sound fun," he said, smiling. "Reags?" He shifted his gaze to Reagan, who sat at the end of the table. She lifted her eyes to meet his without moving her head.

"Fine," she said, her voice monotone.

Thick silence hung awkwardly in the air, exacerbated by the faint scrape of forks against the glass plates. Cora tried her best to focus on what was happening around her, but she was stuck in a whirlwind of her own thoughts about the compass.

"Has anyone seen Max's compass?" The words tumbled out of her mouth before she could stop them.

There was a collective flinch from everyone at the table at the mention of Max's name.

Julie's voice wavered. "I..." she started, blinking quickly. "I actually don't remember." Cora saw wheels of panic begin to churn in Julie's mind. "Ned?" Her mother's eyes darted to her father, and Cora suddenly regretted mentioning the compass at all. Ned stammered before answering. "Y-yeah, I don't know...." His sentence trailed off, and he shook his head.

Julie looked at Cora across the table quizzically. "Why do you ask?"

Cora swallowed hard. She had never overtly lied to her mother, but she also didn't know how to explain what she'd found. Moreover, having Max's keepsake connected her to Max, made him feel close. Cora wasn't willing to give that up.

She shook her head, a flush rising to her cheeks. "I was just thinking about it," she said. "I was looking at the crystal web in my room earlier and it reminded me of that trip to Sedona."

Tears welled in Julie's eyes, and Cora saw Ned place a hand on his wife's, a silent gesture of support. Memories were painful reminders, a blindsiding force that tackled them all, leaving a grief-stricken wreckage in its path. Cora caught Reagan's eye and saw a spark of emotion she couldn't place. Reagan's eyes were cold and harsh. Anger? More than anger. Something darker. The four of them sat in silence, unable to recover from Cora's question.

"Can I be excused?" Reagan asked. She didn't wait for a response but stood immediately. She grabbed her plate and turned from the table before anyone could object.

Cora heard the clink of the glass plate on the counter, the soft thud of Reagan's feet climbing the stairs.

"Me too?" Cora asked, quickly. She looked at her parents expectantly. Silently, her feet bounced underneath the table. She was fidgety and eager to further inspect the compass upstairs.

Julie started to nod, and Cora bolted from the table. She was halfway up the stairs when she heard an audible, "Yes," from her mom.

Chapter 5

NESTLED IN THE COMFORT of her bed, Reagan mindlessly flicked through her phone. In a small digital square, she saw her soccer friends, huddled together at a teammate's house for their weekly team dinner. They had invited her, of course, but Reagan had ignored the invite, just like she had every other invitation. They would get the hint. In the first weeks after Max's passing, friends and teammates had come by with flowers and treats, offerings of condolence. At first, Reagan was embarrassed to admit she welcomed the attention. Everyone preening over her and checking in. Her phone rarely stopped buzzing with notifications. She had even gone to soccer practice the day after, but mid-practice, she realized she had grabbed a pair of Max's soccer socks instead of her own, and she broke down in a heap in the middle of the field.

She hadn't set foot on a soccer field since. She had no desire. It was unlike her, too. Soccer, and her friends, had been her whole life. She was an undisputed star on and off the soccer field. Colleges and universities from across the country were vying for her to play for them. Friends and boys alike adored her, fawning over her every move. Even teachers seemed entranced by her, excusing missed assignments and letting her retake exams without question. Reagan walked the halls of her school confidently. She had sleek, long blond hair that somehow always looked styled. She was slender, her muscles toned from years of playing competitive soccer. Reagan looked just like Julie.

But now when she looked in the mirror, she hardly recognized the reflection staring back at her.

Reagan flopped her phone down onto the bed next to her and looked up at the ceiling. She was sad, of course. Only a terrible person wouldn't feel sad about the death of a sibling. But she was also mad. Max had robbed her of her idyllic senior year. A soccer scholarship awaited her after graduation, and Reagan had been counting down the days until she packed her bags. She wanted adventure and she wanted more room to explore, both figuratively and literally. And then, that day in September had happened, and Reagan's entire world—her entire identity—had crumbled. She'd held her whole glittery world in the palm of her hand, and suddenly it was ash, the charred remains slipping through her fingers.

She heard a commotion down the hall. Drawers were being opened and closed, and she heard rustling. *Probably Cora,* Reagan thought, rolling her eyes at the mere thought of her younger sister. Why did she have to bring up that compass at dinner, anyway? No one even missed that dumb compass except Cora.

Reagan stalked down the hallway to Max's room. With a fierce fury, Reagan flung open the door and was shocked to see, of all people in the family, Julie. She was hunched over Max's nightstand, frantically pulling the contents out. Books and sheets of loose paper were strewn around the room, and piles of clothes littered the floor.

"Mom?" Reagan asked.

Julie turned, tears streaming down her cheeks. They dripped from her chin to the floor and Julie made no attempt to wipe them off before she buried her face in her hands and let out a guttural sob.

"His compass," she sobbed. "I hadn't thought of it until Cora brought it up at dinner, and now I can't find it. I don't think he was buried with it, so it has to be here somewhere!"

Julie turned back to the nightstand and resumed her frantic search. Rage, hot and fiery, boiled in Reagan's stomach. She was furious at her younger sister for dredging up that compass, for bringing up Max so flippantly at the dinner table. She was angry that of the two siblings she had, she was left with Cora.

"Mom," she started again, but she was at a complete loss for words. Reagan could barely hold her own grief in her hands, let alone her mom's. "Let me get Dad," she mumbled, turning her back and leaving her mom in a heap on the floor.

Chapter 6

CORA SMOOTHED THE SHEETS of her bed, then pulled the compass from her pocket. The sight of it in her hand was foreign at first, but the longer it sat, the more it seemed to belong. It fit nicely, resting on the soft pad of her palm. It felt like she was holding magic.

Her fingers navigated the intricacies of the compass, the embossed gold detailing, the mark on the underside. What were the odds of someone else having the same compass, with the same dent on the back?

Cora's door flew open. Reagan stood, glowering from the hallway.

"Just thought you should know," Reagan hissed, jabbing her finger down the hall. "That your stupid question at dinner has left Mom in a crying mess in Max's room. Don't do that stuff anymore, Cora. Don't bring Max up like that." She turned on her heel and stomped down the hallway.

Cora flushed and a wave of guilt and regret washed over her. Reagan was right. It was selfish of her to bring up the compass so abruptly at dinner, but she hadn't been able to help herself.

Out of the corner of her eye, Cora saw the cheery yellow bag Mia had dropped off. Pushing herself off her bed, she went to the bag and retrieved the sketch pad. It was brown and leather-bound, with a long string to keep it all contained. Max and Reagan had always been more comfortable on courts and on fields, exhibiting their athletic prowess. But Cora, she was more comfortable with a pencil in hand, sketching and drawing.

She'd started sketching when she was only five, when Max was taking a beginner art class. She wanted to try because Max did, but she quickly found she loved it. And not only that, her sketches were actually pretty good.

She preferred pencil, able to erase any imperfections. But this time, she sketched without erasing. Her lines were harsh at first. Thick, dark angry marks traced the page and matched her emotions. But the more she drew, the more the anger dissipated. Her lines were loose and light. She let the pencil guide her, letting the lead flow through the pencil onto the paper. When she paused, she was surprised to have drawn a forest with stretching trees and dense leaves. Cora sat in stillness, intrigued. Usually when she let her imagination run wild, the result was a mystical animal or a whimsical doodle. She hardly ever drew landscapes.

This thicket was unfamiliar, unlike anywhere she had ever been. She looked at the trees and the leaves, wondering where that inspiration had come from. She could tell where she had started the drawing—the dark pencil lines at the base of the trees. The lighter strokes were all towards the tops, the delicate edges of the leaves, the detailed blades of grass.

Cora's eyes stung with exhaustion. Maybe a small cat nap wouldn't hurt, she thought, climbing under the covers and nestling into her bed, her fist wrapped around the compass.

Before her head hit her pillow, Cora had fallen fast asleep.

Chapter 7

CORA BREATHED IN AND cool, crisp air filled her lungs. Cool air? Her eyes shot open. Lush green grass surrounded her, sprinkled with dew. She sat up, her breathing shallow. She whipped her head around, trying to make sense of where she was. The ground beneath her was hard, covered in long strands of emerald grass. Tentatively, she put her hand out, grazing the grass with her fingers. Drops of dew lingered on her open palm. The grass was real. Her other fist was clenched tightly around something hard. She opened her hand to see the compass. The compass? She pocketed it quickly.

She craned her neck and looked toward the sky. Sunlight filtered through a canopy of dense leaves. A forest? Cora took a few deep breaths, trying to steady her racing heart and head. The leaves behind Cora rustled, and her blood ran cold. A hand, and then an arm emerged from behind a tree. She was paralyzed, unable to breath or move.

When the figure emerged from behind the tree, Cora blinked, unable to believe her eyes. She wanted to run but she was frozen in place. She wanted to cry, but she couldn't actually believe who was standing in front of her.

It was Max. He started walking toward her, smiling. Cora tried to move again, but she couldn't. She was terrified and transfixed and while her brain was telling her body to move her body wasn't receiving the messages.

Max sat next to her, so close their knees were almost touching.

"Cora," he said softly.

She looked into his eyes, searching for explanation. They were his eyes. That deep, welcoming shade of brown. Her gaze drifted from his eyes to his head, to the mop of brown wavy hair atop his skull. His cheeks were pink and full of life.

"Is this a dream?" she whispered, tears filling her eyes. "You're... How can I see you?"

Max nodded a small nod. "Not a dream, exactly, no. But, not exactly reality, either," he said. "I can't really explain. I don't know for sure myself." He shook his head.

Cora couldn't believe what was happening. She wanted to ask him too many questions, she wanted to know all the things, but she couldn't seem to formulate words or articulate sentences.

"So," Max said. His legs were folded, his hands clasped, his elbows on his knees. Cora had seen him sit like that thousands of times and had never really taken note. She absorbed every detail, wanting to memorize everything again. "What are we waiting for? Show me this place!"

Cora looked at him, dazed. "What are you talking about? I've never been here before."

Max laughed a hearty laugh. Oh, how she'd missed his laughter. Max had an infectious laugh that filled the room. She wanted to remember that laugh forever, to bottle it up and store it on her dresser, a treasured sound she could replay at will.

"What makes you think I've been here?"

He laughed again, throwing his head back and laughing into the sky. The sun shone on his face, and for a moment, he looked iridescent.

She stared at him, incredulous. "I've never seen this place in my life! I just woke up in the grass and then you came from behind the tree! I don't know where I am or how I got here or what is even going on!" Tears pricked her eyes. The absurdity of this whole situation was getting to her.

Sensing her impending despair, Max raised his hands, his palms facing her. "Okay, okay," he said softly. "Let's check this place out, though. You lead the way."

"Max, no," Cora shook her head. She couldn't believe her brother was asking her to lead the way in this strange forest. She was scared to move, scared to breathe, scared to disrupt this sacred, liminal moment with her brother.

"I guess we can just stay where we are," he said, craning his neck and looking around. "This area is pretty nice." He gestured with his hand around the grove of trees surrounding them.

She shrugged. She was perfectly content sitting with Max, not exploring the rest of the forest. She looked around, surveying her surroundings.

"Do you know this place?" she asked.

"No, not at all." Max shook his head. "Come on," he said, lifting himself up. Cora saw a twinkle in his eye. "Let's do it together."

As they walked, Cora's mind raced. *This has to be some sort of dream,* she told herself. Cool air brushed against Cora's cheeks and the wind whispered through the leaves, creating a soft rustle. She inhaled and caught a faint whiff of pine. Max looked real. Really real. Cora desperately wanted to reach out and hug him, but she didn't know how to hug an... angel? She shook her head, as if trying to dislodge an explanation from her brain.

"You keeping up?" Max asked, looking over his shoulder. Max's long legs covered terrain much faster than hers, and Cora was struggling to catch her breath. Cora's thoughts were ricocheting around her brain like ping pong balls, and her emotions were doing the same. In one breath she thought she would cry and in the same exhale she wanted to laugh and shout for joy. So, no, in no way, shape, or form was she keeping up.

They climbed higher and higher, so high that Cora thought they must be hiking amongst the clouds. The sun arced above them, changing position in the sky as the time passed. Cora paused, noticed her shoe was untied, and knelt in the loose rocks to tie it.

When she looked up, the grandeur of a tumbling waterfall stood before them. The magnitude of the fall took her breath away. Below her, water crashed into a frothy pit. It was deafening standing so close to the cascade. She looked around, taking in the moment with all of her senses. The mist from the falls sprayed her face, her arms. The smell surrounding them was fresh and clean.

Nervously, she stepped away from the edge and loose rocks crunched beneath her feet. The waterfall crashed into a pond below. It was a long drop, and being so close to the ledge made Cora queasy. She looked at Max who stood, surveying the waterfall. He leaned forward, looking over the side of the waterfall. Suddenly, without warning, the loose rocks underneath Max's feet shifted and he flailed, tumbling down into the rushing waters below. Cora's stomach lurched.

"Max!" she screamed, but her words were swallowed up in the sound of the cascading water. She was screaming into an abyss. Her eyes darted frantically, searching for someone to help. She was in a full panic, acutely aware that she was very alone and the only person that could help

Max. She stood at the edge, taking in the steep drop below her.

Cora had never been one to take risks, and she didn't consider herself especially brave. The thought of jumping into the water made her stomach flip. She took a deep breath and reached into her pocket, searching for the compass. Nothing. The emptiness startled her, and the rocks shifted beneath her feet. She slid forward, desperately grasping for anything to catch her fall, but it was of no use. There was nothing to save her, either.

The free fall was terrifying, but strangely liberating. Plummeting through the sky, it was as if time slowed down. Air rushed through her hair, whipped through her clothes. Her red hair swirled wildly around her. Her feet hit the water with a powerful jolt. She pumped her legs and swam with all her strength, breaking the surface with a gasp. She rubbed her eyes, ridding them of the excess water, and looked around for Max. Her eyes scanned the bank of the water, searching.

There. She saw him in a clearing, just past the bank.

Cora paddled her way over to the clearing, pulling herself up onto dry ground. She collapsed in a heap, panting, her breath ragged. When she looked up, the weight of the day caught up with her, the uncertainty of where she was and what was happening. It was a very likely possibility that this was a dream, and she would wake to the awful reality that was life without Max. It was all so overwhelming, and a sob overtook her.

"Cora," Max said, and there was a soft kindness in his voice. "It's okay. It's okay."

"It's not okay," Cora stammered. Her eyes met his. She had so many questions, but she couldn't make herself ask them. She remembered the compass, remembered her empty pocket at the top of the waterfall.

"I-I-I lost something," she stammered. The urgency in her voice was palpable.

Max nodded. "Okay, then let's find it!" Max was always up for an adventure. "What is it?"

Cora hesitated. She wasn't sure how to describe it without giving it away.

"It's like a gold...necklace." She omitted that it was his compass, and ignored the twinge of guilt for lying to him.

"All right," Max said, standing. "Let's get looking. Where did you last have it?"

Cora paused. She knew she didn't have it at the top of the waterfall, but she didn't want to go back up there. She eyed the waterfall, remembering her free fall. Max followed her gaze and said softly, "The longer you wait, the bigger it gets."

"What?" Cora asked, quizzically.

"The waterfall," Max said. "The longer you put it off, it's going to seem bigger and bigger in your mind."

"What?" Cora asked again, frustrated. Max seemed to be speaking in riddles that she couldn't understand. "What do you mean?"

Max gestured with his head toward the waterfall. "The longer you wait, the bigger and scarier it seems. I like to get the worst part out of the way first, but it's your necklace." He shrugged.

Actually, it's yours, Cora thought. She looked away.

He was right, and she knew it. She sighed. "Let's start at the top."

They both looked up, wondering how exactly to get back to the top of the waterfall. Max looked at Cora, waiting. Her cheeks heated. They could go the way they had the first time, but the climb was tiresome and time consuming.

"Cora, you can do this," Max encouraged her. Max had always been her biggest cheerleader, and she couldn't stand the thought of leaving this dream, of leaving him.

She took a deep breath, steadied herself. She scanned the perimeter of the pond, searching for a way up. Her eyes caught sight of a thick, green vine, loosely resembling a rope. *No,* she thought. *Absolutely not.* She kept her gaze moving, but she kept tracking back to that vine. She glanced at Max. He smiled, knowingly.

"W-well," she stammered, her voice faltering with uncertainty. "Maybe we could climb that vine over there?" She looked at Max for validation.

"If that's what you want to do, let's do it." Max said.

"Is that what you would do?" she ventured, probing for encouragement.

"It doesn't matter what I would do," he said, his eyes twinkling. "This is about you. This is about what you decide to do."

Cora shifted her weight between her feet, stalling.

"Cora, here's the thing. Sometimes you just have to try a few different things before finding something that works. So maybe the vine will work, maybe it won't. But we won't ever know until we try it. Or until we try something else."

Cora nodded. She understood, but it was hard to convince her feet to move.

She remembered Max's advice from just moments before. *The longer you wait, the bigger it gets.*

"Let's go," Cora said, with a confidence she wasn't sure she actually felt. She forced herself to take a step forward before she could change her mind. She made her way to the side of the waterfall and yanked on the vine. It was thick in her hand, and she half hoped it would fall to the ground with her tug. But it seemed secure.

"How tall do you think that is?" Cora asked, craning her neck to the top of the waterfall. Standing in front of the rock slab, the climb somehow looked even higher.

Max looked up. "Maybe twenty, thirty feet?"

Cora nodded, trying to swallow the fear rising in the back of her throat. "Here we go," she mumbled, taking the vine between her hands. She tried hoisting herself up, using her arms to lift her body, but it was impossible.

"Use your feet, Cor," Max encouraged her.

She leaned back and planted her feet against the rock slab. Her arms shook with exertion and nerves. The white soles of her sneakers were now a pale green, dyed from the lush, damp grass. Her shoes were heavy, soaked from the plunge in the waterfall. With every step up, water seeped from silver eyelets of her sneakers.

Her first steps were shaky and uncertain. She stepped, then once her feet were secure, moved her hands up, inch by inch. Her arms shook; she wasn't sure if it was from muscle fatigue or panic. Either one was equally possible. *Keep going,* she told herself. *Don't look down.*

"You've got this!" Max called down from below. "Just keep going. Focus on your steps. Focus on your breathing."

Cora exhaled loudly, surprised to realize she'd been holding her breath. *Breathe. Step. Adjust hands. Breathe. Step. Adjust hands.* Cora fell into a cadence, focusing on her rhythmic movements. Her hands ached, her grip strained from holding the rope so tightly. She wondered what she had been thinking, assuming she could climb this vine to the top of a waterfall?

"You're almost to the top!" Max yelled. She lifted her eyes and saw the edge of the waterfall, just feet above her. A few more steps and she'd be there!

Breathe. Step. Pull. Breathe. Step. Pull. By her estimation, two more steps and she would be at the top. She smiled and looked down. Seeing the distance to the ground, seeing Max as a speck so far below her, made her stomach flip. She tried to regain her composure, but her next step hit a mossy patch, and her foot slipped. She held onto the vine using only the muscles in her arms to hold her steady.

"Cora!" Max exclaimed. The startled fear in his voice made her panic even more. Her arms were exhausted of all strength, and her grip was fading. "Cora," Max said again. "You've got to pull yourself up. If you can't get your feet to the rock, you need to climb the vine using your arms."

Cora dangled, helpless, strength waning with every passing second.

"If I climb up at the same time, the vine will snap. You need to get to the top before I can come up there," Max called from below.

Cora looked to the summit. It had seemed so close just moments before, but now, it looked insurmountable.

"Cora," Max called again. His voice was loud, clear, and calm. "Follow the same steps as before. Breathe. Then climb. Breathe. Then climb."

She took one breath, then another. With every passing second, her strength diminished. But with her third breath, she found new resolve. Whatever this moment was —a dream, a vision—she couldn't let any time with Max go to waste. She exhaled and pulled herself up. And then she did it again. And then she was close enough to the top that her knees knocked against the wall as she pulled herself up, scraping her shins the entire length of the pull. She crawled further onto flat land before collapsing, breathing hard. And then, she saw it. In the mist of the waterfall, the familiar gold sheen of the compass. Her heart leapt, and she lunged for the compass, clasping it in her fist. The cool spray of the waterfall misted her face one last time before everything went black.

Chapter 8

THE AIR SURROUNDING CORA was warm, and when she moved, the weight of a blanket engulfed her. She knew, without opening her eyes, that she was home. Her heart ached. It was cruel to dream something so real.

Her hands were clenched, balled into tight fists. She peeled back her fingers, revealing the golden compass. The sight of it, and the freshness of the dream, brought real tears to her eyes. She had no idea what time it was, but the house was quiet. Dim, early-morning light peeked through her curtains. She threw the covers back and swung her legs over the edge of the bed. Her pink sneakers were still on her feet. She looked closer. The soles were tinted a pale green. Cora reached out to touch them and found they were damp. She retracted her hand quickly, her heart thumping. Cora pulled her feet closer to examine the shoes more closely, and a sharp pain seared her shins. Giant scrapes traced from her knees to her ankles. She gasped. *From the waterfall,* she thought.

She closed her eyes, trying to make sense of what was happening around her, what was happening inside her head. She tried to think back to what she could remember. The last thing she remembered was grabbing the compass. Before that, she had been with Max.

Cora heard the opening of cupboards and muffled footsteps in the kitchen. Desperate for some normalcy, she shot from the bed and swung open her door, moving downstairs quickly. Her shoes squished with each step. She stepped into the kitchen to see her dad, a bathrobe tied loosely around an old T-shirt and basketball shorts.

"Cora," he said, looking up. "Morning." He eyed her, looking concerned. "Everything okay?" He crossed the kitchen to the stair landing.

"Huh? Yeah, fine. Why?" Cora lied. She was clammy, beads of perspiration along her hairline.

"You're pale." He touched the back of his hand to her forehead, still searching her eyes. "But cool as can be." He turned, heading back into the kitchen. "You want some breakfast?" He opened the refrigerator, peering inside. He made a few disapproving clucks before closing the door. "What about a donut run?" He reached for his car keys.

Cora was ravenous and she welcomed the distraction from her strange morning. Plus, she loved donuts. It had been a tradition to get donuts every Saturday morning, but one that had gone by the wayside since Max's death.

"What do you say?" Her dad was at the garage door, keys in hand.

"Are you going to change?" Cora asked sheepishly.

He looked down, assessing his outfit. "Right, yes," he said, turning to the stairs. "Then donuts?"

Cora waited in the quiet kitchen, feeling guilty for asking her dad to change. But he reappeared quickly, wearing running shoes, a worn pair of jeans, and a souvenir T-shirt from a family trip to Monterrey.

He pointed the direction of the garage. "To the car!" he exclaimed.

They walked to the car, and Cora slumped in the passenger seat, buckling her seat belt. A news radio show sounded from the car speakers. With one hand, Ned awkwardly fumbled with the radio, trying to find a station. "What do you want to listen to?" he asked, glancing at her as he backed out of the driveway.

"Whatever." Cora shrugged.

Ned flipped through satellite stations, landing on a children's pop station. He looked in her direction for her approval, and Cora, not wanting to make her dad feel silly for choosing a children's station, smiled and nodded.

The music gave them both a welcome distraction, and soon they were at the donut shop, standing in front of the glass cases.

Ned tapped his fingers lightly on the glass, examining the sugared pastries and glazed delicacies

"Let's see. We need a glazed donut for Miss Cora, and obviously some maple bars," he said absently. They both noticed his mistake at the same time. Maple bars were Max's favorite donut. The pain in Ned's expression was obvious. He pursed his lips together and closed his eyes, mentally willing himself not to cry in a donut shop. Cora looked away. Her stomach twisted, seeing her dad in that moment. His pain, his sadness was so blinding it was like she was looking directly into the sun. She gave him a quick smile, and then walked to the side of the store that housed the pastries.

"Actually, let's skip the maple bars today," he said quickly, his voice husky. "Chocolate bar, blueberry crumble." He was talking quickly, picking the first donut he saw. "That coconut one looks good. A few sprinkles. Oh, and a plain, glazed donut." He smiled at Cora, and Cora couldn't help but wonder if her taste in donuts was reflective of her personality. Plain, mundane, boring.

He glanced at the other end of the store and motioned to Cora. "Anything else look good?"

"I think Reagan likes the chocolate ones with chocolate frosting," she offered, pointing to a cocoa-colored donut dripping with dark chocolate frosting.

"Oh yes, good memory," he said, nodding. "Let's add a few of those and we should be good!"

On the drive home, she studied her dad's face. She noticed how tired he looked; deep lines were etched around his eyes. He must have sensed her looking at him, because he turned and smiled.

"Hey," he said, patting her hand from the driver's seat and smiling. "Thanks for coming with me this morning. That was fun." Cora smiled back. The drive to the donut shop had been quiet, full of awkward silence as they struggled to find their balance. They were all the same people, but there seemed to be an invisible, Max-shaped wedge between them all now that Max was gone. It was as if he had been the glue that held the Jones family together.

"So." Her dad broke the silence, clearly trying to reestablish the casual rapport from a few moments ago. "Mom said Mia dropped off some art supplies? That was nice. Are you still liking drawing? I noticed it's been a bit since you've shared any of your work on the fridge."

"Yeah, it was super nice of her." Cora said, nodding. "And yeah, I guess. I don't know. I haven't really felt like drawing lately. But I still like it."

Ned nodded, slowly, flicking his turn signal to steer the car onto their street. Cora could tell he was thinking, choosing his next words carefully. He pulled the car into the driveway and pushed the garage door opener but put the car in park. He turned so he was facing Cora.

"I understand that," he said. "I haven't felt like doing a lot of things lately either. Maybe those interests will come back, and maybe they won't. Grief..." He paused. "The loss of a sibling is a big thing, Cora. I hope you know that Mom and I are here if you ever want to talk about anything. Anything at all."

Cora nodded. She knew. The problem was she didn't want to talk about anything. And drawing? Well, she didn't know. Max had been the first one to show her how to draw. She learned by watching his pencil strokes and watching his movements. He showed her how to shade and contour, and when her natural talent for drawing increased, and even surpassed his own ability, he was the first to encourage her. Now, drawing left her with a gnawing in her stomach and a lump in her throat.

"I know, Dad. Thanks." She smiled at him. She wanted to change the subject, and quickly. "Donut time?" she asked.

Ned nodded, shifting the car and pulling into the garage. "Donut time," he said.

Chapter 9

REAGAN CRACKED HER EYES open and squeezed them shut again. Sunlight filtered through her drawn curtains, airy pillars of gauze that hung from a curtain rod. The beaming white of her walls reflected the sunlight, making her room a bright box. Her cheerful yellow bedding now seemed to mock her mood.

She reached an arm from her cocoon and retrieved her phone from the charger. 11:17. She ignored the green icon of a chat bubble, alerting her to new text messages. She didn't care who they were from. She let the phone fall beside her and closed her eyes again, willing herself to fall back asleep. Reagan's phone buzzed lightly next to her. Chalk the text messages up to nine. Another buzz. And another one right after. Someone was calling her.

She glanced at the string of numbers. It wasn't anyone in her contacts. She hit the red X, declining the call. Her caller ID told her the call came from North Carolina, and Reagan didn't know a soul in North Carolina.

She settled back underneath her covers and closed her eyes again, ready for a sleepy reprieve when footsteps thudded down the hallway outside her room. Reagan rolled her eyes. She knew it was Cora.

Flashes from the night before replayed in her mind, and anger simmered inside her. Why had Cora brought up that stupid compass, anyway? It had sent their mom into a frenzy, tearing Max's room apart. Reagan missed Max, for sure. But she missed how things used to be even more. She wanted her old life back, her old routine, her old normal. This was not the way she envisioned her senior year. She had seen herself excelling on the soccer field, ruling the high school halls, signing with a Division I university for their soccer program. She was looking forward to senior trips, and senior days, and now, even though those things would still happen, she actually didn't care about them anymore. She was mad at Max for that. She was mad at him for stealing her senior year. She was mad that her mom and dad were so preoccupied now that the mere mention of anything related to Max unhinged them.

And then there was Cora. Reagan's life was so full before Max died that she almost forgot Cora existed. Now her little sister was almost unbearable. Everything she did annoyed Reagan. Her frizzy red hair drove her nuts. *Straighten it!* Reagan thought, every time she saw it.

Reagan had glossy blond hair and sun-kissed tanned skin. Cora's frizzy red hair took over her head, and her skin was so fair, the pale blue hue of her veins peeked through. She was timid, indecisive, and unsure, while Reagan was confident and determined, sure of what she wanted and how to get it. Cora was the opposite of Reagan in nearly every way imaginable, and Reagan wondered if that was why she had such little tolerance for her irksome younger sister.

Reagan threw off her covers, exasperated at the mere thought of Cora. She had fallen asleep in running shorts and a tank top, even though it had been weeks since she had actually run. She flung her door open, and there sat Cora, on the top of the stairs, tying her stupid pink shoes.

"Of course, I knew those loud footsteps were yours!" She spat her words like venom at Cora. "If you could just try, even the littlest bit, to be less annoying, we would all really appreciate it!" She hissed the last words at Cora, then turned quickly on her heel and slammed her door shut.

Chapter 10

CORA SLUNK DOWN THE stairs, trying not to cry. Her mom met her at the bottom of the stairs, arms open and ready for a hug. Hot tears seeped from Cora's eyes.

"She hates me," Cora said, collapsing into sobs in her mother's arms.

"She doesn't," her mom said, trying to reassure them both. "She's just dealing with things in her own way, maybe."

Her mom held her in her arms, smoothing her hair.

"I have an idea," her mom said. "Want to call Mia? We could go get a bead kit. You guys could make some new bracelets."

Cora sniffled and nodded.

Her mom grabbed her phone from the counter, her thumbs moving expertly to find Mia's mom's contact information. She handed the phone to Cora.

"Give her a call and see if she's free," she said.

Cora was overjoyed when Mia was free, and they excitedly made plans to get a new bead kit and make bracelets back at Cora's house.

The busy morning had been a distraction, but on the drive to Mia's house, Cora found it was hard to concentrate on anything but her dream. *But dreams don't leave bits of grass on your shoes,* she thought. Sleepwalking? Cora wondered. *But your shoes were wet.* There it was again, that pesky inner voice interrupting her thoughts.

Mia had always been Cora's best friend, for as long as she could remember. There had never been secrets between the two, until yesterday. She decided she would tell Mia about the compass and the dream. Maybe her friend could help.

"Cora?"

"Huh?" Cora asked.

"We're here, honey. You seemed pretty lost in thought there for a minute," Her mom's voice was gentle. "Everything okay?"

"Yeah, fine," Cora responded, reaching to unclick her seatbelt. "I'll be right back." She opened the car door and hopped out before her mother could say anything else.

She walked to the front door and rang the doorbell. She stood on the porch, suddenly aware that she wasn't sure what to do with her hands. They were clasped awkwardly in front of her, so she dropped her hands and tried folding her arms. But that wasn't right either. She stuffed them in her pockets. Suddenly a breathless Mia pulled open the door.

"Mom! Cora's here! See you later!" Mia called into the house, and stepped on the porch, pulling the door shut behind her. "Hey," she said to Cora, as they stepped off the front porch and headed to the car. "How's it going?"

Cora shrugged. "Fine, I guess." She would tell Mia about Reagan, about her blowup, later. And she would tell Mia about the dream. *For sure,* she told herself. She would for sure tell Mia about her dream.

"Hey, Mia!" Julie turned from the driver seat and greeted Mia, who was climbing into the backseat of the car.

Mia's mom emerged from the house, waving from the porch. Julie and the two girls waved back and reversed from the driveway.

Inside the craft store, the girls beelined to the jewelry section. They stood in front of the beads, admiring the selection.

"Which one should we get?" asked Cora.

Mia looked from side to side, taking inventory of the kits they already had. She pulled two from the shelves. "I don't have either of these, do you?" She held out a kit filled with every color of the rainbow, in nearly every size imaginable, shaped like little chevron tiles. They were designed to fit nicely inside each other. In her other hand, she held out an alphabet tile kit—little white beads with black letters, so they could string together letters and words.

"Let's do the alphabet!" Cora exclaimed. She had seen some girls at school wearing alphabet bracelets, bearing the names of their best friends or their boyfriend.

"That's what I was thinking, too." Mia nodded, and Cora noticed her glasses slip down the bridge of her nose with each bob of her head. Mia pushed them back into place with one finger.

The trip home took no time at all. As soon as Julie put the car in park, the girls scrambled from the car, heading straight for the stairs.

"Hi. Bye," Ned joked, waving from the kitchen island.

"They have new beads to make," Julie explained, following the girls into the kitchen.

"I'd like a bracelet with my name on it, please," he called after them.

Mia laughed, and Cora smiled. "Okay Dad, sure thing," she said.

They made their way upstairs. Cora held her index finger to her lips as they passed Reagan's room, making a "shh" motion. Down the hall a few steps and they were at Cora's room. They made themselves comfortable on the floor, then opened the bead kit. Cora grabbed a pair of scissors from her desk, and once their supplies were organized, the girls got to work, stringing beads one at a time.

"Is Reagan sick or something?" Mia asked, threading a cobalt blue bead. The bracelet she was working on had varying shades of blue, accented by little gold beads in between. "Why did we have to be quiet?"

Cora shrugged. "I don't know what's going on with her." She paused, reaching for an emerald green bead. "This morning, I was putting my shoes on at the top of the stairs, and she came out of her room and just yelled at me. She said I was too loud, but I wasn't even loud. Anyway, my mom said she is just dealing with stuff in her own way. I don't know. She mostly stays in her room. She only comes out when my mom forces her."

Mia nodded, holding her bracelet up and inspecting her pattern of blues. "Weird," Mia said, and Cora knew it was for her benefit, but she appreciated it anyway.

"Yeah, it's weird," Cora agreed. "She hasn't even wanted to play soccer. Like, she really just stays in her room, all day long."

When she looked up from her bracelet, Mia was watching her. Her brown eyes were soft, and they looked a little sad behind her glasses.

"Are you okay?" Mia finally asked.

Cora tried to swallow the lump that was quickly growing in her throat. "Yeah, I'm fine," she smiled, trying to reassure Mia. Before the veneer could crack, she changed the subject. "Let's make a matching bracelet!"

Part of her hesitation in answering Mia's question was that she didn't really know how she was doing. Some moments of the day, she was fine. Sometimes she even forgot that her life had changed, that her brother had died. But sometimes, most of the time, a thick cloud of sadness hung over her, following her every move. She didn't like talking about it, though. Especially not right now. She just wanted to make bracelets with Mia and have one of those moments where she just forgot.

Mia's eyes lingered on Cora, and Cora shifted uncomfortably under her friend's gaze. She busied her hands, worried Mia would keep asking her questions. She pretended to inspect her bracelet. Mia took the hint, and after a slight pause, agreed to the matching bracelet.

"What colors should we do?" Mia asked. "And what should it say?"

Cora ran her hands over the beads, watched how they turned over as her hand passed. The deep green reminded her of the lush forest from her dream, and beads of perspiration popped onto her palms.

"We could do yellow and orange?" Cora suggested, noting that neither of them had used those colors.

"Oh yeah, I love that idea," Mia said, nodding her head in excitement. "And let's use these metallic ones between them!"

"Cool!" Cora exclaimed, relieved that Mia had seemed to move on from the conversation about Max. "But what should it say?"

Mia looked at the beads of letters, grouping letters to see what they could make. "What about MCBFF?" she asked. "Mia, Cora, best friends forever?" She arranged a group of letters and showed Cora.

Cora nodded, "I love it!" She separated yellow and orange beads into piles for her and Mia to pull from.

"Hey, have you ever had like, a really crazy dream?" She kept her gaze focused on the beads in front of her, careful to avoid eye contact with Mia.

"Like a nightmare?" Mia asked.

"No, like it just felt so real. Like you're sure you were awake, but you were dreaming?"

Mia thought for a bit. One of Cora's favorite things about Mia was how she not only heard, but she took time to thoughtfully consider and answer honestly. Cora could tell Mia was really trying to remember if that had ever happened to her. Suddenly, Mia brightened.

"Oh! Like when you dream you're going to the bathroom, but then you wake up and you really do almost go to the bathroom?"

Cora was crestfallen and hoped her disappointment didn't show on her face. "Yeah, kind of like that," she replied, continuing to search for beads and keeping her head down.

"What was your dream?" Mia asked.

Cora paused. Here was her opportunity to share her dream with her best friend. She had promised herself she would, but now, faced with it, Cora suddenly realized how crazy it sounded and couldn't bring herself to share.

"I can't even remember," she finally answered. "I just remember waking up and feeling like I had been somewhere else."

"Dreams are so weird," Mia said.

"Oh, thank you for the sketch pad!" Cora exclaimed brightly, seizing the opportunity to change the subject once more. "I started using it last night. It's been a while since I've been sketching, but last night it felt good."

"No problem. It was my mom's idea," Mia admitted. "Why haven't you been sketching?" She asked Cora, picking through beads to finish her bracelet.

Cora shrugged. It was an innocent question, but Cora wasn't sure of the answer. Days and weeks had passed, and still Cora didn't feel like picking up a pencil. She remembered what her dad said in the car and wondered if she would ever feel like drawing again.

"Maybe now you'll feel like it more often," Mia said. "You're such a good artist."

Cora's cheeks flushed with embarrassment at the compliment.

"Thanks," she said, then changed the subject. "Did you guys have fun on your trip?"

"Yeah, it was fun. My mom kept talking about how close we lived to all these national parks, and how we never saw them," Mia said. "We went to these things called slot canyons. The walls are so high and a crazy, bright red color. It's insane. I'll show you a picture when you drop me off. It's on my mom's phone."

For a moment, Cora was jealous of Mia's family trip, but then she remembered how awkward things were with her family right now, and she couldn't imagine spending hours in the car with them all. Their last vacation was the Grand Canyon, when Max got his compass. Cora swallowed hard, the memory bringing tears to her eyes. She blinked quickly, willing them to disappear, and this time it worked.

She cleared her throat before she answered. "Cool! I want to see it."

The girls worked silently for a bit, stringing beads and knotting string. It seemed like they had just started when Cora heard a knock on the door.

"Girls?" her mom called from the hall. "It's probably time to get Mia back home. I told her mom she'd be back in a few hours."

"Okay!" the girls called in unison.

There were a bunch of yellow beads leftover, and Cora had strung them together haphazardly. She found herself searching for the letters, R-E-A-G-A-N.

She shook her head in disbelief. *No way, not after this morning,* she thought. But she strung them on quickly and placed the bracelet on her desk.

"Thanks for coming over." Cora smiled at Mia, extending a hand to help her friend up. "That was really fun." And she meant it.

"I love our bracelets," Mia said cheerily. She held her wrist out and rotated it, moving it in small circles and examining the stack of beads. She motioned with her head in the direction of Cora's desk. "I saw you make that one," she said. "You should give it to her. Maybe it would help."

Cora shrugged. "Maybe. Or maybe it would give her something to throw at me."

They opened Cora's door, careful to pause their conversation and tread lightly as they passed Reagan's door.

Chapter 11

"ALL RIGHT, SO HOW was the bead kit?" Julie asked. She glanced at Cora in the passenger seat, and then shifted her gaze to Mia in the back.

"It was good!" They answered in unison, erupting in peals of laughter.

"Let's see the goods." Julie quickly pulled her eyes from the road, long enough to glance at the bracelets adorning their small wrists. Mia held her arm up in the backseat so Julie could see in the mirror. "I like them!" They pulled into Mia's driveway, the car rocking gently as Julie put it into a parked position.

"Thanks for having me!" Mia gathered her few things from the backseat.

"Thanks for hanging out. It was so fun," Cora said, turning in her seat to face Mia.

"So fun," Mia agreed, dragging out the *O*. "I'll see you Monday?"

"See you Monday," Cora said.

Julie and Cora waited in the driveway until Mia had closed the garage, waving until the door shut and she was no longer visible.

"I had a lot of fun, Mom," Cora said. "Thanks for the idea."

"I'm glad you did," Julie said. She reached over and patted Cora's arm. "It feels good to see you and Mia together like that, having fun, hanging out."

Julie's phone buzzed.

"Oh, that's Mia's mom," she said, glancing at the small square screen. "Will you see what she said? I wonder if Mia forgot something."

Cora tapped into the message from Mia's mom. "Oh," she said, opening to a picture. "Mia was telling me about these crazy canyons they saw on their trip. She said she would show me when we dropped her off."

Julie looked over quickly, catching a glimpse of a steep, copper canyon. "Wow," she said. "Those are really something. Where is that?"

Cora nodded. "Yeah, I think she said it was a slot canyon or something?" Cora's eyes were glued to the screen. She used her two fingers to zoom in and out, focusing on different parts of the canyon. The canyon walls were steep; from the picture, Cora couldn't even see the top of them. Mia stood in the middle of the canyon, barely squeezing through the opening. Her small frame looked even smaller in comparison to the colossal, sheer rock. Her hands rested on either side of the vibrant copper canyon wall.

"Mom, these are insane." Her gaze was still glued to the electronic square in front of her. "How do things like this even exist?"

Julie glanced at the phone in Cora's hand. "I think it takes years and years of water running through them," Julie replied.

"Can I look it up on your phone?" Cora asked.

"Only if you tell me about what you find," Julie replied with a teasing smile. Cora deftly navigated the phone's internet browser, quickly tapping the keys.

"Whoa," Cora said, awestruck. "These canyons are amazing." She flipped the screen so Julie could see more easily. Cora looked at a few more pictures before turning her attention to an article describing the formation and location of slot canyons.

"You're right," she said finally. "It takes millions of years. Millions! But they're formed when water rushes down them. So cool. We should go see them sometime."

"Let's add it to the list," Julie said. They neared their driveway.

Cora nodded. "Yeah, that sounds really good, Mom. Thanks." Cora smiled at Julie.

But a sense of dread settled over Cora as they entered the house. The afternoon had been so nice with Mia, so... normal. But the Jones's new normal was still fragile. So fragile that, at times, Cora thought it might crumble, eroded away like the rock in the canyons.

Chapter 12

CORA SWIVELED ON A stool in the kitchen, watching her mom make dinner. She was happy to be helping her mom in the kitchen. Cora remembered being younger, and everyone crowded around the kitchen island, watching as Julie cooked. As Reagan's soccer schedule intensified and Max busied himself with student government and a variety of practices, the audience eventually dwindled to just Cora. She savored the time alone with her mom, with nothing to break her mom's focus or attention. She found the ramen on the shelf and handed it to her mom.

"Thank you, sweetie," her mom said, briefly looking up from chopping herbs. Water boiled on the stove. "Can you put them in the water for me?" She motioned to the pot of bubbling water.

Cora removed the sheets of dry ramen noodles and dropped them in the water, watching the heat break them apart. She kept the flavor packets on the side, unsure just what her mother did with the spices.

"It seemed like you and Mia had a really good time," her mom said, a knife moving rhythmically in her hands.

"Yeah, we did," Cora replied. She stirred the curling noodles with a wooden spoon, her thoughts lost in the swirling pasta.

"What did you two talk about up there for hours?"

Cora's stomach twisted. *Well, we didn't talk about my weird dream,* she thought. She really had planned on telling Mia. She had tried, but she just didn't know how to explain such a strange circumstance. She glanced at her shoes, as if they could give her an answer. All traces of the night before were gone, and she wondered if she had been in a fog in the early morning, thinking she was awake when really, she was still dreaming. *But it was so real,* she thought. And the compass. *The compass!* Cora's stomach rolled. She wasn't even sure where she had put it after realizing her hand had been clenching it in her sleep.

"Just school and stuff, I guess," Cora replied vaguely. "Mom, I need to check something in my room. I'll be right back." She set the wooden spoon down and ran up the stairs. As soon as she entered her room, she saw it. The gilded amulet had a special shine. Her eyes were drawn to it, wherever it was.

She grabbed it from her nightstand, tucking it into her palm and scanning her room for a safe place to put it. She saw the stretchy cord from the bracelet-making kit she and Mia used earlier. She cut a long piece, strung the compass on it, and tied it tightly around her neck. She tucked it underneath her shirt, glancing in the mirror before heading downstairs. It was hardly noticeable, hidden beneath layers of clothing. Donning the talisman connected Cora to Max in a way she couldn't articulate.

She saw her sketchpad and pencil on her bed and grabbed it before heading back downstairs.

"Everything okay?" Julie asked as Cora entered the kitchen. She was slicing chicken, tilting the cutting board and using the knife to guide it into the pot of simmering ramen noodles.

Cora nodded, setting the sketchpad and pencil on the kitchen island and resuming her spot at the barstool.

"Do you still need help, or can I draw for a while?" She opened her sketchpad to a new page.

"I think everything is pretty much done here," Julie said, looking around the kitchen. "I'm glad to see you're putting that to use. You're such a talented artist."

"Thanks, Mom. Can I see your phone?" Cora looked up, adopting a hopeful expression. "I want to try drawing those slot canyons."

Julie grabbed her phone from the counter and handed it to Cora. As the pencil touched the paper, Cora let loose, letting the lead of the pencil guide her. She was consumed by the steep, arching lines of the slot canyons.

"Cora?" A familiar voice broke her reverie. "Dinner's ready, honey."

She looked up to see her mom with bowls of steaming ramen balanced in her hands.

"Right. Coming." Cora said. She slid off the barstool and walked toward the kitchen table. She was already counting down the minutes until she could resume her sketching. She touched the compass against her chest. Everything was just where it should be.

Chapter 13

CORA WAS LITERALLY THE last person Reagan wanted to see, but she couldn't ignore the gnawing hunger in her stomach. A delicious scent wafted up the stairs, and it reminded her that she hadn't eaten all day. She threw off the duvet cover and swung her legs over the edge of the bed. Her thigh flattened against her mattress. She poked the top of her leg, noting that her athletic legs were quickly losing muscle tone. *Oh well,* she thought, standing and raising her arms above her head in a stretch. She yawned and lowered her arms, stretching her back and hamstrings. Her muscles were tight and rigid.

Reagan glanced at herself in her mirror before leaving her room. Her blond hair was messy and matted. At one point, it had been in a bun on top of her head, but she really couldn't remember when she had last brushed it or washed it. She wasn't even sure when she had brushed her teeth last. She ran her tongue over her teeth. *Whatever,* she thought. She opened her bedroom door and descended the stairs. Cora's back was to her, hunched over and scribbling on a notepad. Her mom stood at the stove, slowly stirring a pot. Reagan's stomach rumbled with hunger. Her mom looked up and smiled.

"Hey, honey!" She chirped brightly.

At their mom's voice, Cora looked up, her eyes darting from her mom to Reagan.

"Is dinner almost ready?" Reagan asked, standing at the edge of the island.

"Almost," her mom replied, keeping Reagan's gaze longer than was comfortable. "What have you been up to today?" Her tone was conversational, but Reagan wasn't up for small talk.

"Sleeping," she said shortly. She glanced at the sketchpad. "What are you doing?"

"Drawing," Cora replied. She didn't lift her head, but Cora drew her elbows in and hunched her shoulders over, drawing herself inward as if trying to make herself even smaller.

"Well obviously, nerd," Reagan said. "But *what* are you drawing?" She peered over Cora's shoulder as Cora frantically tried to cover up her sketches. "I can't even tell what that is. You should probably keep practicing because that's not very good," Reagan sneered.

"Reagan!" Her mom snapped, and when she met her mother's eyes, they were serious. "You cannot talk to your sister like that. You can't take your anger out on Cora. It's not fair. You're not the only one who is sad. Your life isn't the only one that has changed."

Reagan flinched, stunned at the outburst from her mom.

"Sorry," she mumbled to Cora.

If she hadn't been so hungry, Reagan would have retreated to her room for the night. But she was hungry, so she pacified herself with the apology and plopped on the couch, scrolling through her phone to distract her.

Great, thought Reagan. *Literally the worst time of my day begins.*

Chapter 14

SCALING RED CLIFFS AND canyon walls consumed Cora's thoughts as she sketched at the kitchen island. She frowned at the lines on her sketchpad, dismayed.

"Mom? Can I use the computer to look at some pictures of more canyons?" Cora asked.

"Of course," Julie replied. She set a soapy bowl in the sink and looked over her shoulder at Cora. "You're pretty enamored with those canyons, huh? They are really breathtaking."

"Yeah," Cora admitted. "They're just so cool."

Cora opened an internet browser and typed in 'slot canyon.' Images of stunning orange canyons popped up. The beauty of the steep, steep walls and narrow openings was fascinating. She clicked on each image, taking in the variegated lines, deep rust fading to pastel pinks and oranges. Some pictures showed people in the canyon, miniature figures posed against massive canyon walls.

She devoured information about how the canyons were formed by millions of years of flash floods—sudden bursts of raging waters that swept through the canyon. She read of hikers that had been killed as the unexpected surge of water raced through the openings, some as narrow as ten inches. Cora blinked, imagining ten inches. She didn't know if she could squeeze through an opening that small.

Cora was mesmerized by the canyons and clicked article after article, image after image.

Her mom appeared at the office door, and Cora jumped with surprise.

"How's the research going?" she asked. A dish towel was thrown over her mom's shoulder, and she leaned against the doorway.

"These are amazing," Cora answered, turning her attention back to the screen.

"They are something else," Julie agreed. "It's hard to believe something that stunning was created naturally."

Cora nodded, still clicking through images.

"Which one is your favorite?" her mom asked. She stood behind Cora now.

"This one," Cora replied, instantly. She pulled up an image of the first canyon she had seen. A copper canyon filled the screen, with walls so high the top wasn't pictured. The V-shaped canyon narrowed at the bottom, soaring into near vertical slabs of rock. Pastel pink lines accented the deep rust walls that curved and sloped, a result of eons of water coursing through them.

"Wow," Julie muttered, clearly struck by the picture. "They really are breathtaking."

Julie stroked the top of Cora's head. *Taming the wild frizz,* Cora thought.

"I don't want to interrupt your research, but I was thinking we could watch a movie or something?"

But Cora was itching to draw more. "Can we watch tomorrow? I really want to draw these canyons."

"Oh, sure," her mom replied. Cora tried to ignore the disappointment in her mom's voice. "Tomorrow it is." Julie planted a quick kiss on the top of Cora's head.

"I think I might actually go upstairs," Cora said. She yawned, suddenly overcome by exhaustion. How long had she been researching?

"Okay," Julie smiled. "I'll be up in a bit for bedtime."

Cora gathered her pencil and sketchpad, memorizing the intricacies of the canyons. Walking up the stairs, she was careful to be especially quiet as she snuck past Reagan's room. At her room, Cora flopped onto her bed. She kicked her shoes off, reminded of her dream from the previous night.

That was such a weird dream, Cora thought. The further away she got from the dream, the more convinced she was that it was just that, a dream. As she changed into pajamas, she made sure the compass was tucked safely underneath her shirt. She liked keeping it close to her heart.

Cora brushed her teeth alone in the shared upstairs bathroom. It was strange to have the bathroom all to herself. There was one bathroom upstairs, which meant Cora had always shared with Reagan and Max. Reagan normally spent nearly all her time at home in the bathroom, styling her hair, contouring her face with varying shades of makeup, spritzing fragrance. There'd hardly been room for Cora or Max.

As she brushed her teeth, Cora thought about how rarely Reagan had been in the bathroom lately. Cora spotted Reagan's hair brush on the bathroom counter and wondered the last time her sister had even brushed her hair. When Reagan had come downstairs for dinner, Cora had hardly recognized her. Her normally polished sister looked disheveled, with crumpled clothes and tangled, matted hair.

She finished brushing her teeth, turned off the light, and left the bathroom. She hesitated for a fleeting moment outside Reagan's room. She remembered the bracelet she had made for Reagan earlier that afternoon. But just as quickly, she remembered Reagan's rage the night before about the compass. She remembered how Reagan had snapped at her earlier that afternoon, how she had teased Cora maliciously before dinner, and Cora changed her mind.

Back in her bedroom, Cora settled herself on her bed. She laid on her stomach, head propped on one hand, sketching light lines. Mia had told her that the bottom of the canyon was almost all sand, making walking a challenge at times. Cora shaded lightly, giving the appearance of a narrow sand walkway between the canyon walls.

With each stroke of her pencil, her eyelids sank lower and lower. Her head bobbed as she dozed off. She tossed her sketchpad to the floor, climbed under her cozy comforter, and fell fast asleep.

Chapter 15

A TRICKLE OF SWEAT ran down the back of Cora's neck and along the sides of her face. Cora opened her eyes. She gasped, and hot, stifling air filled her lungs. She knew exactly where she was. The sand, the scaling, rust canyon walls. She scrambled to stand, her feet sinking slightly. Red sand clung to the soles of her shoes.

Cora walked, following the trail through the canyon walls instinctively, tracing her hand along the red rock. She came around a corner and there he sat, perched on a rock. Max waved, and Cora scrambled up the rock to sit beside him.

"This place is cool," he said, looking up along the walls of the canyon.

"It's really cool," Cora agreed, lightly tracing her fingertips in the sand. "Mia went on a family trip here, and I thought it was so pretty. I was trying to draw—" She stopped suddenly, a realization fitting together like a puzzle piece coming together in her mind.

"Wait," she said, working through her thoughts out loud. "I was drawing this when I fell asleep, and now I'm dreaming about it. Is that why I'm dreaming about these places?"

"Maybe," Max shrugged, his eyes twinkling. "Maybe not."

Cora didn't want to waste any time.

"Well, we're here. Should we explore?" Cora asked. There was something about being in Max's presence that bolstered Cora's confidence.

He stood and extended a hand to Cora, pulling her from her seated position.

They walked through the beautifully eroded canyon, turning sideways at times to fit through the narrow passageways. Cora held her breath as she squeezed through the first pass, worried that an exhale might wedge her between the steep slabs.

"What's happening with Reagan?" Max asked suddenly, looking at Cora.

"I don't even know where to begin," Cora said quietly. "She never comes out of her room, and when she does, she's just really mean." Cora remembered Reagan's harsh words and her cruel eyes. Cora retold the story, leaving out the part about the compass from a few nights ago. She touched the spot on her chest where the compass hung. Still there.

They walked a few steps in silence, and Cora wondered if she had shared too much. When he responded, his voice was different, husky and thick.

"I'm sorry that happened, Cora," he said quietly. "It sounds like she's having a hard time," Max said.

A stab of resentment pierced Cora, and tears stung her eyes at his answer. She wanted to exclaim that they all were going through a hard time. That losing him had left a Max-sized hole in all their hearts. That he had been the one who kept everyone together. Now, without him, Cora worried they would all come unglued, like astronauts who lost their tether, drifting further and further apart, floating alone in their own little silos.

But she said none of that. She nodded in agreement.

"Cora, I know you're all going through the same thing," he said, as if reading her mind. But Reagan—" He paused and cleared his throat. "Be the bigger person, Cora. You'll never, ever regret being kind to someone, even if they aren't kind to you. And we know, Reagan can be unkind to you." He looked back at her and smiled.

"I don't want to be the bigger person." Cora knew how childish it sounded. "She's just mean, Max, she is. And she takes it all out on me." Her face contorted into a pout.

"She can be mean," Max agreed, nodding. He paused before continuing. "Give her the bracelet and see what happens." He gave her a knowing smile.

"The bracelet? How do you know about the bracelet?" Cora asked. Instinctively, she touched her shirt where the compass was.

Max shrugged and walked ahead, leaving Cora behind him, dumbfounded. As soon as he turned his back to her, Cora hastily removed the compass from her neck and shoved it into her pocket, out of Max's all-knowing gaze.

The sun beat down and beads of sweat trailed down the side of her face. They walked for a few paces in silence, and Cora's eyes drifted to the changing sand below her feet. What had once been dry sand was now pocked with puddles.

"Wow," Max said quietly, as they approached a majestic waterfall. Cora looked ahead. The water cascading down the red rock wall had an eerie, silver-like sheen to it. A haphazard ladder—a fallen tree with boards nailed as steps —was perched to the side of the cascading water.

"Are we climbing up that?" Cora asked, gesturing toward the ladder with her head.

Max looked at the ladder, looked back at her and shrugged. "I don't know. Are we?"

"What's up there? Past the waterfall?" She asked, squinting her eyes.

Max shrugged again. "I don't know. I've never been here before either," he said, smiling. He walked forward, his feet trudging through ankle-deep water. Cora looked at her own feet, submerged beneath murky water. She shifted her weight from side to side, wondering if what was on the other side of that waterfall was worth the risk.

Max stood to the side, his hands on his hips, admiring the natural beauty around them. Cora stepped to the ladder, lifted one foot, and set it gingerly on the first rung. She lifted herself and bounced lightly, testing the stability. The ladder shifted, and Cora's stomach lurched. She hopped off quickly.

Max laughed. "Well, now you know what to expect if you want to try again. But if not, that's cool too."

Cora turned back to the ladder. She put one foot in front of the other, slowly and deliberately, her hands moving in tandem with her feet. She climbed with a confidence that surprised her, and when her fingertips touched a pool of cool water, she knew she was nearing the top. She pulled herself up and looked back down at Max, triumphant in her ascent.

"Are you coming?" she called down with a smile.

Max let out a buoyant laugh that carried up the canyon walls, and Cora's heart surged. She missed that laugh. He scrambled through the water to the base of the ladder, ascending easily.

"How did you do that so fast? Weren't you scared?" Cora asked, as Max reached the top.

He looked down below him, nonchalantly. "Not really," he replied, swinging his legs over the top of the ladder. His feet landed in a shallow pool of water, making a small splash. They looked ahead to another makeshift ladder, if another propped tree with a few boards nailed in could be called a ladder. A rope hung down the side of the wall. The sun was hot above them, and Cora's arms were sore from the strain of the first climb.

"Can we take a break for a second?" she asked, shielding her face with her arms. She squinted in Max's direction.

He nodded and waved his hand to one side. "There's an overhang. Let's get out of the sun."

They waded slowly through the ankle-deep water until they reached the shade of the overhang, a welcome reprieve from the blistering sun. Underneath the overhang, the canyon wall sloped up slightly, so there was a space to sit out of the water. They plopped onto the sand and Cora exhaled loudly.

"That was really brave of you, Cora," Max said, nodding toward the top of the ladder.

"I was still scared," she said quietly.

"That's what being brave is, Cora! It's facing something you're scared of and doing it, anyway."

Cora thought of the easy way Max had scaled the ladder, exuding confidence.

"Why can't I be more like you and Reagan?" she asked quietly. It was a question she pondered often, wondering why she had to be the shy one, the quiet one, the non-athletic one. Everyone had their *thing*. Reagan had soccer.

She was beautiful. She had hordes of friends. Max had been good at everything, friends with everyone. Cora was still searching desperately seeking her *thing*.

"Everyone has something," Max said, softly. "Sometimes it just takes time to figure it out." He waited for her response. When she didn't answer, he continued. "The world doesn't need another Reagan, or another Max. The world needs Cora. And the best version of Cora you can be."

She shook her head. "I don't want to be Cora," she insisted. "I want to fit in. I want to have friends. I want to be good at something..." She trailed off, realizing how silly she sounded.

"You have friends, Cora," Max said.

"Friend," Cora said, emphasizing the singularity of the word. "Friend. Not friends, just one friend."

"One single friend that cares a lot about you, though," Max replied. "How many of Reagan's friends have you seen come over lately?" he asked.

Cora reflected on the question posed by her brother. Actually, come to think of it, she hadn't seen any of Reagan's friends lately.

"It's not about how many friends you have, Cora," Max continued. "It's about the real friends you have. You can have all the friends in the world, and still feel like the loneliest person in the room." Max was looking straight ahead, but Cora could tell he was speaking from experience. His voice was thick, and he rubbed his eyes slowly.

It was true that Mia was the best friend Cora could ask for, and she was grateful for Mia's friendship. But she saw troupes of girls walking down the hallway at school, girls who had friends in every class because their friend circles were so large. She heard them talking about upcoming plans and who would go to whose house, and she yearned to be part of those groups. She wanted to belong somewhere.

Cora craned her neck to see the top of the second, towering waterfall that dwarfed the first waterfall in height and size.

"How tall is that?" Cora asked.

"It's tall, but you've done it before. Are you ready to give it a shot?"

She nodded and pushed herself off the ground. At the ladder she hesitated, shifting her weight between each foot.

"You've done it before, and you can do it again. That's half the battle, convincing yourself you can do something," Max said earnestly.

The longer you wait, the bigger it gets, she thought. She stepped forward. Grabbing the rope, she put her foot on the ladder and began her ascent. The climb was treacherous, but it was easier than scaling the waterfall in her last dream. She knew she wasn't physically stronger, but something about it was easier. Her footing was more secure, each step bolstering her confidence. She climbed for a few minutes, and she looked up. The view ahead was disappointing as she realized she was less than halfway to the top. She looked down and instantly regretted it. The muscles in her arms strained with each second that ticked by. Her body swayed on the ladder.

"Cora!" Max called from below. "Focus on the step right in front of you!"

Cora took a deep breath, steadying herself and refocusing her mind. One foot in front of the other. *Focus on what's right ahead of you.* One step and pull. Another step. *You can do this,* Cora told herself. *Keep going, keep climbing.* If she looked ahead, if she thought about what was ahead of her, she wasn't sure she could keep going. The distance, the feat overwhelmed her. But she knew she could manage one step.

She followed Max's advice and focused on the step right in front of her. Beads of sweat dripped down the sides of her face and her palms were wet with perspiration. Her arms were drained, her grip on the rope loosening with each pull. *You've done this before,* she reminded herself. One foot in front of the other. With one last pull, her eyes scanned the ledge. She had made it to the top. She pulled herself up over the last step, her arms shaking and hands weak.

She rested her hands on her hips and looked around, taking in the beauty of her surroundings and catching her breath. The cliffs around her soared into the sky. A few feet ahead the canyon narrowed, just like in Mia's picture. The sun disappeared and Cora peered into the sky to see a cloud had covered the sun, offering her a reprieve from the heat. She was so captivated by her surroundings, she didn't notice Max standing right next to her.

"Pretty amazing, huh?" he said.

"You scared me," she gasped, looking at him. She was tempted to reach out and touch his arm, but she also didn't want to risk disturbing anything around them, as if he were some sort of hologram and touching him would disturb the waves of light.

"Let's check it out," Cora said, wading through the water toward the funneling of the canyon. A surge of pride coursed through her body at her own courage.

They waded through the water, hitting first their ankles, and then their shins, their knee caps, until they were nearly waist deep. Cora tried to ignore her anxiety about the murky water. She spread her arms, both sides of the canyon pressed against her palms. She turned around to make sure Max was following close behind. He smiled, encouragingly. The landscape around them was breathtaking. Next to the vibrant copper walls, the water took on a jade-green tint. The canyon narrowed even further a few yards ahead. Cora's pulse quickened, fear rising into her chest and throat. Not knowing what was beyond the canyon walls made her uneasy.

Max whistled as the narrowing came more into view. "Look at that."

Cora gauged the canyon walls. They were narrow, but if they turned sideways, they could get through. *But how long is it that narrow for? And what's on the other side?*

"What do we do?" he asked. "Keep going? Or turn around?"

"I d-don't know," Cora stammered. "We could fit if we turned sideways, but what if it goes on like that for a while? And we don't even know what's on the other side..." She trailed off, uncertain.

"Yeah, those are good questions." Max said patiently.

"Well, what do you think?" Cora asked.

Max looked at her, and Cora saw the kindness in his gaze. It had been a long time since she looked into his eyes, and the act of it made her blink away sudden tears.

"Cora, what's wrong?" he asked, quietly.

"It's just, it's just not fair, Max. It's not." Cora was crying now, her narrow shoulders shaking.

"What's not fair?" Max asked, even quieter this time.

"All of it. It's not fair that everything is different, and I don't know if it will ever be the same." She was hysterical, unable to stop the tears from streaming down her face.

"It won't be the same, Cora," Max replied quietly.

She looked at him, waiting for him to continue. "Then what are we supposed to do?" It was a genuine question. Cora didn't know how to do life without Max. She didn't know how to help her parents; she didn't know what to do with Reagan.

"I don't know, Cora," Max said finally. "I don't know how to help you guys. That's something you each need to figure out on your own."

She was deflated. She'd hoped Max had golden words of wisdom for her. Her sadness was jarred by a cold, wet drop splashing her shoulder. Another one hit her forehead.

"Did you feel that?" she asked, rubbing her head where the raindrop hit.

Max nodded and held his hand out, palm facing up, gauging the rain. His mouth was pulled down into a tight frown. Rain pelted their skin and the soft pitter-patter of the drops hitting water filled the canyon.

The rain fell quickly now, and in a moment of sickening realization, Cora remembered just how these canyons were formed: tons of water coursing through the canyon in powerful flash floods had carved the canyon walls. Now, Cora and Max were caught in a rainstorm that could very quickly turn into one of those floods.

Cora's eyes scanned the canyon walls, reaching fifty, sixty, seventy feet in the air. She couldn't be sure. It was pouring now, and Cora had to wipe her eyes to keep the rain water out.

Max's eyes followed Cora's, scanning the top of the canyon walls.

"What do we do?" Cora asked, her voice panicked. She desperately tried to recall bits and phrases from her research on slot canyons. The waist-deep water had risen already, hitting just below Cora's rib cage. Her breaths were shallow and fast. She took a deep breath and tried to steady herself. "Think, Cora," she told herself under her breath.

Get to high ground. She remembered the tip from an article she had read. Cora frantically scanned her surroundings. There was no way to get to high ground; the canyon walls simply weren't scalable without equipment, and there was no way to make it through the narrow canyon. It was too dangerous. They needed to move quickly; it wouldn't be long until they were submerged.

"We need to try to wedge ourselves somewhere," Cora said finally, recalling a story she had read about stranded hikers that had survived a flash flood by wedging themselves between a rock and the canyon wall. "At least it will keep us from going over the edge." She looked in the other direction, her eyes trailing over the edge of the waterfall.

"There's a rock!" Max pointed to a rock a few yards ahead. It looked big enough to hold both of their feet. It was easier to swim than walk by now, and Cora cringed as branches, dirt and rocks knocked against her legs and caught between her fingers.

Max pulled himself out of the water and reached out a hand to Cora. He pulled her up, and they positioned themselves, their backs braced against the canyon wall and feet planted firmly on the rock. There wasn't much room on the rock, but there was enough.

"I guess we just wait here until the rain lets up?" Cora asked, looking around. She tried not to think about what would happen if room on the rock ran out before then rain stopped.

Max nodded. "Yeah, I guess so."

"And what if it never lets up? What if we get swept away and washed over the side?" It was no use trying to calm her panic now.

"Sometimes the only way forward is to do the next best thing. This is the best thing we can do, right now, with what we have. We'll find the next best thing when we need to."

A peal of thunder cracked through the canyon. The echo reverberated and vibrated deep in Cora's bones. The water rose around her, and Cora wondered which would come first: her legs tiring to a point she couldn't hold on any longer, or the water sweeping her away. She pushed her back harder against the canyon wall.

Sheets of rain poured from the ominous, grey sky. There was another loud crack, followed by the low roar of rushing water. Cora looked just in time to see frothy white rapids tumbling out of the slot canyon.

Max looked at her. "Cora, just go with it. Hold your breath, and flow with the water." He gave her a confident nod.

Cora nodded, watching the wall of water rushing toward her. She looked down into her lap, trying to steady her breathing. She noticed a small bulge in the corner of her pocket. The compass! If she went over, the compass would fall out in the water, and she would never find it again. She shoved her hand in her pocket and wrapped her first around the compass, right as a wall of water crashed into her.

Chapter 16

CORA WOKE WITH A jolt, and her surroundings jolted her even more. She was in her own room, canopy bed and all, and she was sopping wet. She looked down at her closed fist. There sat the compass. Her fist had been clenched so tightly, a deep imprint where the compass had been remained in her palm. She sat, bewildered. Once, she could chalk up to a dream. But twice? She had a sudden realization that maybe this was all one big figment of her imagination. The first sequence of events, the forest, the donuts, the bracelet making with Mia and the slot canyon... all one big fantasy. That must be it. She would wake from this strange delusion in the morning.

She moved her hands over her arms, feeling the grit of the fine, canyon sand underneath her hands. Red dirt covered her bed, her clothes. Her hands shot to her head, feeling the granules embedded in her hair. She was eager to shower, to rinse off the layer of silt covering her body. She stood and peeled each layer of clothing off, watching a cloud of copper dust settle around her.

The house was usually eerily quiet. Reagan scrolled absently. Her eyes flicked to the clock. 3:37 a.m. No one else was awake in the middle of the night. No one but her. The sudden sound of rushing water from the bathroom startled her. Someone was awake.

Reagan threw the covers from her body and bolted out of bed. Her adrenaline was pumping, and it was the first time in weeks she felt something, any sort of emotion besides apathy. Quietly, she opened the bathroom door, overcome by humid heat. *Who is showering at this time of night?* she wondered. She closed the door quietly and tiptoed back to her room, staking out the hallway. There was only one other person who used that bathroom, but Reagan couldn't imagine why Cora would be showering in the middle of the night. *Because she's the weirdest human alive?* She rolled her eyes.

Reagan waited patiently for the shower water to stop. A few minutes passed, and the shower went quiet. Reagan lifted her head. This was the moment she had been waiting for. The door opened slightly, and Cora's small body, wrapped tightly in a light pink towel, emerged from the bathroom.

"Why are you showering in the middle of the night?" Reagan demanded.

Cora gasped and jumped backwards.

"Reagan!" Her voice was loud in the quiet hall. "You scared me!"

"Shh!" Reagan hissed, looking over her shoulder in the direction of their parents room. "Well?" Reagan waited.

"Well what?" Cora asked.

"Well, what are you doing, showering in the middle of the night?" She spoke slowly, enunciating each word.

"I-I couldn't sleep," Cora stammered. "And I figured maybe a shower would help." Cora pulled the towel tighter around her body, accentuating her small frame.

Reagan shook her head. She didn't believe that Cora thought a shower would help her sleep, but she didn't know what her sister was up to.

"Can I go get dressed now?" Cora asked quietly, trying to skirt around her sister.

Reagan kept her feet planted firmly in front of Cora, forcing her younger sister to squeeze by.

"I hope you sleep better." She said the last few words in a cooing, singsong voice like she was talking to a baby.

"Thanks." Cora ignored the mocking tone and beelined to her bedroom, closing the door quickly behind her.

Reagan watched her close the door before she went into the bathroom. She didn't know what she was looking for, but she was looking for something, some clue as to why Cora had been showering at this bizarre hour. The counter was undisturbed, toothbrushes and hair brushes strewn about. A gob of blue toothpaste sat in the sink. Reagan pulled the shower curtain open and looked down into the porcelain tub. She squinted. There, at the tub drain, was a small mound of wet, red sand.

Chapter 17

BACK IN THE SAFETY of her own room, Cora exhaled. Her heart was still racing from her hallway scare from Reagan. *Why on earth was she awake at this hour?* Cora wondered, drying her body with the towel and changing into a pair of oversized sweats and a warm sweatshirt. Her teeth chattered. She was freezing. It was as if the water from the dream had seeped into her skin and settled deep into her bones. She ran a brush through her hair and pulled it into a ponytail. She checked the trinket box, ensured that the compass was safely inside, and dove underneath her comforter.

She curled into a small ball, trying to warm herself. Adrenaline coursed through her veins, a combination of running into Reagan in the middle of the night and the slot canyon. It had been so real, and yet she knew it couldn't be. That world, that dream, walked a fine line between reality and a delusion, a liminal space she didn't know how to explain. The sounds, smells, feelings.

And then, there were the obvious indicators that it actually was real. Like the sand in the tub. Her green-tinged sneakers from the forest the night before. And a dull, sore tightness in Cora's legs and back from physical exertion. She tightened her arms around her legs, her body still cold, and thankfully fell into an exhausted, dreamless sleep.

Reagan stood over the shower and rubbed her thumb and index finger together, examining the fine, orange-red granules. The substance didn't resemble anything from their neighborhood, or anything close by, for that matter. She had never seen sand like that before. She turned on the sink faucet and put her hand underneath the steady stream of water, watching the flecks trail down her fingers and swirl into the drain. *Where had it come from, and why was Cora showering at three in the morning?* Reagan squinted suspiciously at her reflection in the mirror.

Her sister was up to something. Something strange, for sure, if it involved Cora. And Reagan was determined to get to the bottom of it.

Chapter 18

"CORA? IT'S TIME TO get up." Someone was rubbing her back. Cora cracked her eyes open and saw her mom sitting on the edge of her bed. She stretched beneath a pile of blankets, sore muscles flexing and tensing.

"What time is it?" Cora asked, rubbing her groggy eyes.

"Almost seven thirty. How did you sleep?" Julie stroked Cora's hair.

Cora recoiled quickly, remembering her damp hair from the shower, but it was too late. Julie already noticed.

"Did you shower last night? Your hair is wet," she asked, her eyebrows pulled together in a frown.

"Oh, yeah. I couldn't sleep and thought a shower might help." Her stomach twisted as she retold the lie. She hated lying to her mom. She turned away, avoiding her mother's gaze. "I should probably start getting ready for school."

From her peripheral vision, Cora saw the pile of wet clothes in a clump by her bed.

Julie stood from the bed and Cora saw her mom's gaze settle on the heap of clothes and pause. Cora waited for the questions to come. But instead, her mom stepped over the clothes and walked to the doorway. She turned back to Cora.

"Breakfast is ready when you are," she said with a smile and left the room.

Cora waited until the door clicked softly behind her mom, then exhaled a sigh of relief.

Cora heard Reagan's pounding footsteps on the stairs before she saw her. *How ironic*, she thought. She braced herself. Surely Reagan would bring up the shower.

Reagan's face came into view, a menacing smile plastered to her face.

"Reagan! Good morning, sweetie," her mom said cheerily, spooning waffle batter into the hot iron. The batter sizzled. "You're up early." Her mom glanced at the clock on the microwave. "Your classes don't start until later today."

As a senior, Reagan rarely had to be at school. As a graduating student athlete, she was required to be enrolled in at least one class, but between testing out of classes and advanced placement classes, Reagan was only at school for a couple of hours each week, allowing her to sleep in almost every morning.

Reagan ignored their mom and kept her eyes focused on Cora.

"I know. I guess I couldn't go back to sleep after someone was up showering all night." She emphasized the word "someone," carrying up the last syllable in a singsong voice. "Tell me, why exactly did you need to shower in the middle of the night?" She was at the barstool next to Cora, her eyes piercing like daggers.

Heat raced up Cora's neck and onto her cheeks. She swallowed, trying to buy time. But Cora didn't need to come up with an answer.

"Reagan," Julie warned, shooting a harsh look at Reagan.

Reagan ignored her.

"Hmm? Cora? Tell us why there was a bunch of sand in the shower, if you just showered to help you fall asleep."

"Reagan!" Julie interrupted. "You cannot talk to your sister like that. I've had it up to here with how you've been treating Cora." She raised her hand, palm down to her eyes to demonstrate her level of frustration with Reagan. "It's not nice, and right now, we can all use a little more kindness." She said the last word deliberately, and her voice cracked just a little bit.

Reagan gave Cora an icy stare before retreating.

"Sorry," she mumbled quietly, and looked away.

"Don't apologize to me," Julie said, flipping the waffle maker over and extracting a browned waffle. She placed it on a plate and pushed the plate across the kitchen island to Cora. "Apologize to Cora." She stood, her hands on the counter, looking expectantly at Reagan.

"Sorry," Reagan huffed, glancing over her shoulder in Cora's direction. "I'm going back to my room." She slid off the island barstool and up the stairs.

Julie watched her, calling, "Waffles are down here if you decide you're interested." She looked at Cora. "I'm sorry," she said, softly. "I'm sorry for Reagan, and I'm sorry I haven't done something about that sooner." She looked down, tears spilling onto her cheeks.

"It's okay," Cora said. She swiveled on the barstool and rounded the island to her mom. Cora hated to admit it, but she was grateful to Reagan. It seemed the interaction had distracted her mom from the question of the sand in the shower. *Thanks, Reagan.*

"I haven't been the kind of mom I want to be," Julie whispered into Cora's hair, her arms wrapped around Cora. "I've been so consumed with Max and..." At the mention of Max's name, her mom's body shook with sobs.

The thought of Max and the sight of her mom in such distress made Cora's eyes sting with tears. "I get it."

Her mom held her shoulders and pushed her back gently, looking at her face. "We're going to be okay. We're going to get through this," she said, nodding with each word. Cora wasn't sure who her mom was trying to convince of this fact—herself or Cora.

"I love you so much," her mom said. "So, so much."

Cora nodded. "I love you, too, Mom." A moment later, still in a tight embrace. Cora said, "Mom? I kind of need to get ready for school."

"Oh! Yes, of course," Julie relaxed her grip and pulled away. "I guess school is still a thing we should probably do. Hurry upstairs and get changed. I'll get your lunch ready."

Cora reached to pull her waffle from her plate.

"I'm going to take this with me," she said, grabbing a bite before heading up the stairs.

Chapter 19

EVEN THOUGH SHE HAD been in classes for months now, middle school was still foreign to Cora. She had been dreading middle school since she learned that in middle school, classrooms switched almost every hour and included a stop at a locker in between to switch school supplies. Different books for different classes. For months during her fifth-grade year, and the summer before middle school, Cora stressed about not being able to open her locker during the brief switch period. She panicked about getting lost, not being able to find her classroom and being marked tardy.

So, she had practiced. Day after day, she and her mom—and sometimes Max—went to the empty school. Her mom showed her how to fiddle with the locker: left, right, left, then lift the lever to open. Max showed her the classrooms, and they had a practice rehearsal, walking from each classroom to her locker, to the next classroom, over and over and over again. When she couldn't get the last number of her locker combination memorized, Max gave her a helpful memorization tactic.

"If you can't remember the last number, just remember, it's the same day as my birthday. Twenty-one," he said, smiling.

On the first day of school, Cora's nerves overtook her, and after a few fumbles, she realized she had completely forgotten her locker combination. She desperately searched her pockets, frantically trying to find the slip of paper with the numbers on it. The number of kids in the hall dwindling, the bell would ring soon. Her palms were sweaty as she simultaneously tried to find the paper and wracked her memory for any recollection.

"14-7-," she muttered under her breath, before remembering Max's trick. His birthday! She spun the lock to 21 and pushed the lever up. It opened, and Cora nearly cried with relief.

That was the first day of school, and as her mom and Max assured her, it did get easier and less stressful with each day. Now, she had no problem opening her locker, but every time she spun the numbers on the lock to that last number, she thought of Max.

Julie pulled the car to a stop in front the school. "All right," she said, putting the car in park and pulling her sunglasses from her face. "Have everything?" She reached behind the passenger seat, searching for anything Cora left behind.

Cora nodded and swallowed. She didn't want to leave the cocoon of her mom's car.

While the routines of middle school had become easier, the actual act of being a middle schooler had not. Cora had Mia, but she was painfully shy around others, blushing when a teacher called on her, or when someone jostled her in the hallway. Now, she saw people cover their mouths and whisper secretly behind their hands when she walked by. Her teachers looked at her for a moment too long, sadness in their expressions. She preferred being ignored, being invisible.

"Cora?" She was suddenly aware of someone calling her name. "Cora?" It was her mom. "Everything okay, love?" Her eyes were dark with concern.

"Yeah, sorry," Cora said, shaking her head and gathering her backpack. "Thanks for the ride. See you after school. Love you." She smiled and reached for the door handle.

"Love you, bug," her mom said, watching her exit the car. Her mom waited, every day, until Cora disappeared behind the automated doors. Cora gave her a small wave before being swallowed up in the chaos of getting to first period.

The hallways buzzed, chatter and conversations about the weekend filling the bustling hallways. When she spun her locker combination to 21, she thought of Max. The first day back at school after his death, she had broken into a pool of tears when she hit that number, but today, she thought of her dreams with Max. Her locker opened easily, and Cora unloaded her backpack.

Mia appeared at her side, smiling. "Hey," she said.

"Hey," Cora said, smiling back.

"How was the rest of your weekend?" Mia asked, as Cora finished depositing the contents of her backpack into her locker. "Any more altercations with Reagan?" She smiled as she asked the last question.

Cora thought of the shower last night, but she definitely couldn't share that with Mia. Not now, or at least not yet.

She shook her head. "Not really. My mom did kind of get mad at her this morning, though, and Reagan just walked away." She shrugged.

"Your mom got mad?" Mia asked, incredulously. "What happened?"

Cora closed her locker and the two girls walked to their first class together, snaking between students and backpacks. "She was mean to me this morning, and my mom told her it was enough, that she needed to be nice."

"Go Mrs. Jones!" Mia exclaimed.

Cora smiled slightly and nodded. "I just hope it doesn't make Reagan hate me more. I don't even know if that's possible." She shrugged again.

"Yeah, I hope not," Mia agreed. They entered their class and found their seats.

Their homeroom teacher, Mr. Willard, let them sit anywhere they wanted, and Cora and Mia always sat by each other. Cora was thrilled to start every Monday, Wednesday, and Friday by her best friend. Mr. Willard's class was one of her favorites. He taught world geography, and Cora loved learning about different places and cultures.

"Good morning, girls," Mr. Willard said as they walked in. The warning bell rang a few minutes prior, and only a few students were already in the class. Cora and Mia took their seats while Mr. Willard finished final preparations for today's lesson.

Mr. Willard was an older teacher, with light red hair and highly freckled skin. His face flushed easily, and his rotund belly strained against the sweater vests he often wore.

A map of the world hung next to the whiteboard, and Mr. Willard was scrawling big letters across it. N-E-W Z-E-A-L-A-N-D. His blue marker made small squeaks as he went, writing the letters of this week's country across the board. Cora's stomach clenched into a constricting knot.

Every week, they learned about a new country, and normally Cora reveled in it. But New Zealand? She had never been to New Zealand, but she heard about the country every day for years from Max. New Zealand was the top of his travel wish list, and he was constantly spouting facts about the country and what he planned to do there. The room started to spin, and she found herself blinking rapidly to prevent tears from spilling over.

She looked down at her fingers as classmates filed in, thumping their books on their desks. Some laughed, some finished exuberant conversations.

"Hey, Willard!" one yelled, and erupted into laughter.

"Yes, yes, welcome back from your weekend," Mr. Willard said patiently. He turned around to face the class with his hands clasped in front of him, rocking back and forth on his heels. He smiled at no one in particular, and when the bell sounded, he clapped his hands together. "There it is! Let's get started." He turned on his heel and walked to the map.

He pointed to a small cluster of islands toward the right-hand bottom corner of the map.

"Can anyone tell me what these islands are?" he asked, looking around the room. When no one answered, he hitched his thumb behind him to the whiteboard. "There's a huge hint on the whiteboard."

"New Zealand?" someone in the back of the class ventured.

"Yes! New Zealand." Mr. Willard said enthusiastically, moving towards the white board. "This week we're learning about New Zealand. Has anyone been there before?"

He looked out into the classroom. No one raised a hand. Cora was surprised. Usually at least one person had traveled to wherever they were studying. Mr. Willard looked momentarily surprised, too. "Well! I guess we'll all be learning this week, then."

They went through the flag, the history of the country, the imports and exports. Mr. Willard showed a short video, and Cora was entranced. For all that Max had talked about it, Cora had done little research herself. A pang of guilt coursed through her, remorse that she never took an interest is New Zealand until now, when it was too late. It looked beautiful. Steep mountain peaks, rolling green hills, and sparkling turquoise waters. The class went by quickly, and before she knew it, Mr. Willard was switching the lights on and explaining their homework for the week.

"We'll learn about New Zealand for the rest of the week, but tonight, I want you all to research a place in New Zealand you'd like to visit. There are beaches, mountains, tourist attractions, you name it. The terrain is diverse. That's one of the best things about New Zealand. You don't have to do anything with that information yet but take some time to look around the country and see where you would go if you could."

The bell rang as he finished speaking.

"See you Wednesday!" he called as students stuffed loose papers into notebooks, slammed book covers, and hustled out of desks.

Cora and Mia packed up their stuff slowly.

"New Zealand looks cool," Cora said in awe, still envisioning the landscapes they'd seen during class.

"I know. Did you see that water?!" Mia exclaimed. "I know where I'm going. Straight to that beach."

Cora laughed. By now they were at the door, diverging for their separate classes. "It looked so pretty," she said, and gave Mia a smile. "See you at lunch?" she asked.

Mia nodded affirmatively. "See you at lunch."

It was difficult for Cora to focus on her other classes for the rest of the day. Her thoughts kept drifting back to Max and New Zealand. The assignment to research New Zealand was like a fresh wave of sadness washing over her. Max had been so excited about it, ever since he watched a surfing documentary featuring the country's extensive coastlines.

The dismissal bell rang, and Cora walked quickly to her locker. She emptied her books and notebooks into her backpack and found Mia.

"Ready?" Cora asked. Instead of riding the bus both of their parents picked them up from school. Every day they walked to the pickup line together.

"Ready!" Mia said, nodding once. Her glasses slipped down her nose a little bit, and her crop of curly brown hair bounced forward when she nodded.

They weaved between a group of boys playfully pushing each other, and lockers opening and closing. Cora noticed a sign announcing an intramural volleyball tryout. Her eyes lingered on the sign before she pulled her gaze away. She had never played before, but she liked the idea of playing a sport, of being part of a team. As quickly as that thought entered, Cora pushed it out of her mind. What if she didn't make it? What if a ball hit her in the face and she was humiliated? She dismissed the idea quickly.

Cora and Mia walked outside, the bright sunlight momentarily blinding each of them.

Mia spotted her mom's car right away. "There's my mom," she said, and started walking towards the sage-green Subaru. "See you tomorrow!" Mia waved over her shoulder. Her backpack looked as big as she was, bouncing on her shoulders. The passenger window of the car was rolled down, and Mia's mom called, "Hi, Cora!" She smiled behind sunglasses and gave Cora a friendly wave.

Cora waved back and scanned the pickup line for her mom. She spotted her mom's car a few cars back and walked to the car.

"Hey, honey!" her mom said as Cora opened the door.

Cora climbed in and slid her backpack off her shoulders. "Hi, Mom."

"How was school?" Julie asked, glancing over her shoulder before exiting the pickup line.

"It was good," Cora shrugged a little. She considered telling her mom about the volleyball tryouts, but decided against it. She also decided not to mention New Zealand to her mom. She wanted to spare her mom the sadness she was feeling, the heaviness of it bearing down upon her chest.

"Yeah? Just fine?" Julie asked. She glanced at Cora as she maneuvered around the parking lot. "Was Mia at school today?"

Cora settled back in her seat. "Yeah, Mia was there."

The tension in Cora's shoulders dissipated as they drove further from the school. Cora was anxious at school. She worried about saying or doing something to embarrass herself. She had seen the way Max and Reagan talked with friends, and it seemed so easy and natural. Cora was comfortable with Mia, but anyone else and she got nervous. Sweaty palms and one million thoughts swirling through her head.

She had once overheard someone describe her as awkward. She hadn't known what the word meant and had looked it up on the family computer when she got home. The definition stung and stuck with her. It loomed over her every movement. When the toe of her shoes stuck on the carpet and she tripped, her face flushed red and the word *awkward* flashed like a neon sign in her head. When she took too long to answer a question in class, the word swirled in her mind like smoke, infiltrating her every thought.

It was as if that descriptor had attached itself to her, following her every move, haunting her. She worried constantly that her movements, her laugh, even her speech was *awkward*. When she'd heard it from one of Reagan's friends, she instantly knew it wasn't a compliment.

Reagan and her friend had come home from a soccer practice, laughing and tossing their blond hair over their tanned shoulders. Cora had been sitting at the kitchen table, drawing in silence. She sat silently and watched them as they walked in.

Reagan had ignored her, beelining straight for the stairs to her bedroom. Trailing her up the stairs, her friend had laughed and said, "Oh man, your sister is so awkward. I'm so sorry."

Reagan had laughed. "I know. At least you don't have to live with her."

Recalling the experience stung, and Cora winced. She hadn't even been able to tell Max because she was too embarrassed, too afraid he might confirm what they said.

"Cora? Sweetie?" Her mom was calling her now, breaking her from her archived memories.

"Sorry, Mom. What did you say?" She tried to push the memory from her mind.

"I asked if you had a lot of homework tonight," her mom repeated, flicking the turn signal to go left. The car crept to the middle of the road, waiting for an opening.

"Not really." Cora answered. "Mr. Willard gave us a project about New Zealand, but for tonight we just have to decide where in New Zealand we would go if we had the chance." She watched her mom's face anxiously, waiting for her mom's response. Julie grimaced, but kept her eyes on the road.

"New Zealand," her mom said, turning the steering wheel and guiding the car onto their street. "You know Max always wanted to go there." Her voice was soft.

Cora looked at her mom. It was one of the few times she had heard her mom say her brother's name since his death, and his name sounded foreign coming from her lips. Talking about her brother was bittersweet, though for her parents, it seemed mostly bitter.

Her mom looked over at her and smiled, the corners of her mouth turning up. Her eyes were red, and Cora could see tears threatening to fall.

"I can't wait to see where you decide to go," she said, finally. She patted Cora's knee with her hand.

Cora nodded and a small glimmer of relief passed over her. It was as if talking about New Zealand, talking about the project had actually lightened the weight on her chest. A glimmer of excitement ignited in Cora about the assignment. She couldn't help but wonder if Max would meet her there, too.

Chapter 20

REAGAN'S THUMB SCROLLED FURIOUSLY on the glass screen of her phone, her glazed eyes breezing over the square images and puny captions. People living and posting and sharing their lives. That was the thing about grief; her world was shattered around her, but everyone else's world kept spinning. She saw posts from her friends, announcing college acceptances; mundane posts, announcing who they were going to a school dance with. She saw faces, smashed together to fit in one small frame. Jealousy and resentment surged inside her like hot, coursing lava. She was bitter that their lives carried on as usual. That they got to worry about things like where to go to lunch, and Reagan was sitting at home, in bed, worrying that the gnawing in her stomach, that the pain in her heart would never go away. Wondering if she would ever feel like herself again. Wondering what the way out of this darkness looked like.

The sadness that perpetually hung over Reagan was particularly thick today, but she couldn't pinpoint why. Sure, Max was her brother and they had been friendly, but she wouldn't have said they were close, exactly—were any teenage siblings close? Reagan realized maybe her sadness was really regret. Maybe what she was feeling wasn't sadness over what had been lost, though that was part of it, but maybe she was feeling regret, for things unsaid and undone. Maybe she was feeling sadness over things that would never be.

She heard the garage door open and glanced at the screen on the phone. 3:15. It must be Cora and Mom. Cora. Reagan rolled her eyes and a dark thought crossed her mind. It should have been Cora. If anyone had to be taken from their family, it should have been Cora. She was the one who didn't fit in. Max had so much going for him, so much to offer. It should have been Cora.

A string of unfamiliar numbers popped up on her phone screen, interrupting her scrolling and thoughts. The caller ID registered the number as being from North Carolina. She clicked the red X, immediately declining the call. Reagan was declining calls from her best friends; she certainly wasn't going to accept a call from a number she didn't know.

A voicemail notification popped up on her screen. Without listening to the voicemail, Reagan clicked the small blue trash can icon, immediately deleting it.

Chapter 21

CORA TYPED "NEW ZEALAND" into the search bar and the results popped up instantaneously. The juxtaposition of her emotions was stark: a sense of closeness to Max learning about a country he loved so much, and yet a deep sadness that Max would never have the opportunity to visit the country.

She scrolled through the images, waiting for one that caught her attention. There were beaches, mountains, what looked like mountain goats, and lots of people jumping, headfirst, off a tall bridge. Turquoise waters set below rolling green mountains. She kept scrolling. Halfway down the page, she saw it. A majestic archway set atop a glimmering golden beach. Cora clicked on the picture, and a second browser window popped up. "Explore Cathedral Cove" the website read, in blocky white letters set against a black banner. Cora looked at pictures of happy couples, families, adventurers. They all looked happy with exuberant, bright smiles. The families reminded her of what her family used to be, smiling broadly for the camera. She made a note to remember Cathedral Cove and clicked on a small arrow on the screen, taking her back to a page full of images. She scanned, searching for more. The picture was dark, almost black, with neon blue blobs. She clicked on the image, expanding the picture to fit the computer screen. The caption read, "Glowworm Caves." She clicked on the picture again and a booking page popped onto her screen. "Take an enchanting boat ride through an incredible glowworm cave," the booking website read. "See a magical sight of thousands of tiny, shimmering glowworms, and hear the amazing acoustics of the Cathedral."

She squinted her eyes at the images on the computer. Were those really illuminated glowworms? She quickly opened a new tab on her web browser and typed, "How are glowworm caves formed?" and found quickly they were, indeed, glowworms.

"Gross," she muttered under her breath. But she was riveted, too.

She leaned back in the office chair and glanced out the window, surprised to see the light outside was already fading. It was almost dinnertime. Her stomach twisted in knots at the thought of being at the table with her family. Every conversation, every sentence was forced, contrived. Cora knew no one wanted to talk about Max, but in an effort to ignore him, to ignore his absence, they weren't able to talk about anything else.

The door to the garage opened, and Cora heard her dad enter the kitchen. "Hi, sweetie!" he said to Julie. "How was your day?"

"Good." The word came out in a monotone. "How about yours? How was work?"

"Fine. It was just fine," her dad answered. "Where are the girls?"

"Cora's in the office, and Reagan is in her room," her mom replied. The sound of a sizzle came from the kitchen.

"Can I help with anything?"

Her mom didn't respond, and Cora could only assume she was shaking her head no, because her dad then said, "Right, well, I'll just go get changed then." His footsteps thumped toward the office, heading to the stairs.

"Hey, Cor-bug!" he exclaimed, his face appearing at the office door.

"Hey, Dad," she said, looking up from the computer.

"How's the homework coming?" He stood behind her now and kissed the top of her head. "Oh, my. What are you working on? Looks creepy." He pointed to the glow caves on the screen.

"It's a project for world geography," Cora said. "We're supposed to be researching where we would go in New Zealand if we had the chance."

She swore her dad winced at the words *New Zealand*, but he didn't acknowledge it. "Awesome," he said, finally. "I'm excited to see where you choose." He smiled at her before leaving. "I'm going to go get changed. I think dinner will be ready soon."

Cora printed off the picture of Cathedral Cove and the picture of the glowworm cave, then ran them upstairs to her room. She stashed them under her sketchpad, checked to make sure the compass was tucked away in her trinket box, and headed back downstairs for dinner.

Chapter 22

A GENTLE KNOCK CAME from the other side of Reagan's door and her mom's voice floated into the room.

"Reagan, honey?" she said, softly opening Reagan's door. "It's time for dinner."

Reagan's room was swathed in darkness, a sliver of light from the hallway casting a narrow triangle of yellow light on her bedroom floor.

"I'm not hungry," she said with a sigh. She pulled her comforter further over her head, buried herself deeper in her own world.

Her bed sank as her mom sat on the edge of her bed. "I know you don't feel like eating," she said. "But at least come sit with us. I think a change of scenery might be good for you."

Reagan ignored her.

"Reagan, I'm sorry about what happened earlier at breakfast," Julie said, kindly. "But we'd really like you to come down and eat with us, or at least sit with us."

Reagan had forgotten about breakfast, forgotten about her plot to torment Cora until now. Suddenly she had new motivation to sit at the dinner table—to badger Cora.

"Okay, I'll come," she acquiesced, throwing off her covers and rising from the bed. Before Julie could stand, Reagan was halfway down the stairs.

Over a plate of chicken tacos, Ned clasped his hands together. "Cora, how was school today?"

Cora was mid-bite and took a few moments to chew and swallow.

"Good," she said, suspicious of where this might be leading. Since Max's death, the talk around the dinner table had been forced and awkward, and many nights instead of small talk, the family ate in silence.

"Tell me about the best part," her dad said as he held a taco up to his mouth.

"Um," Cora looked at the ceiling, as if searching for an answer from above. "I don't know, probably getting a new assignment from Mr. Willard's class that I'm excited to start." She folded a tortilla around her chicken and lifted it to her mouth.

Reagan scoffed from across the table. "The best part of your day was getting a homework assignment?" She shook her head. "What a sad little life you live."

Julie shot her a look, and Cora's dad moved on quickly, ignoring Reagan's commentary.

"That sounds exciting. Is that what you were working on earlier?" he asked.

Cora nodded. "This is just the first part, so I think there will be more too."

"I can't wait to see what it is," Ned said enthusiastically. "Reagan, what was the best part of your day?"

Reagan checked her wrist, pretending to check the time even though there was no watch. "In about twenty minutes when I can go back to my room and go to bed," she replied. She placed a chip in her mouth and crunched loudly. "Cora," Reagan said, quickly changing the subject. "I noticed there was like, a ton of red sand in the shower after you were done." Reagan smirked at Cora from across the table.

"Red sand?" Julie asked, now turning her attention to Cora. "Where did that come from?"

Cora's chest was tight, her breathing constricted. She didn't have an answer to the question. A believable answer, that is.

Sweat dampened her palms. She chewed the food in her mouth slowly, giving her time to think of an answer. Three sets of eyes sat looking at her expectantly. No one moved. Ned and Julie looked slightly confused, and Reagan looked gleeful. Cora swallowed.

"I don't know," she answered, trying to keep her tone casual and light. "It must have been in my socks or something." She shrugged.

"In your socks?" Reagan echoed. She said the last word slowly, as if making sure she heard Cora correctly.

Ned exchanged a quick glance with Julie. Reagan was never friendly to Cora, but since Max's death, she had turned downright cruel.

Cora shrugged again, her petite shoulders raising an inch toward her ears before dropping them again.

Reagan shook her head. "You're so weird," she said. "Can I be done now?" She rose from the table, pushing her chair back and lifting her plate. She set her plate on the kitchen counter next to the sink and disappeared into the hallway.

After dinner, Cora helped her mom and dad clear the kitchen table, relieved the attention was off her and her late-night shower. She tried, really tried, to think kind thoughts about Reagan, but it was hard. She remembered what Max had said, to be kind to Reagan, that she was struggling more than Cora knew. She pushed the thought away. *I'm struggling too,* she thought stubbornly.

"Thanks for dinner," she said to her mom. "Do you need help with anything else?" She was anxious to get to her sketchpad.

"I don't think so," her mom said, looking around the kitchen. "I'm just going to clean this up and then I'm done. Thank you though," she said, and squeezed Cora to her side and planted a kiss on the top of Cora's head.

"I'll help clean up the kitchen," her dad chimed, and when her mom began to protest, he said firmly, "Julie, I'm helping tonight."

"I'm going to go upstairs to start working on my project for Mr. Willard's class," Cora said. She was light on her feet on the way up the stairs, careful not to disturb Reagan. The last thing she needed was Reagan setting her fiery sights on her—again.

Chapter 23

IN HER ROOM, CORA sat on the floor with her back against her bed for support, the sketchpad propped up on her knees, the pictures of New Zealand unfolded on the floor next to her, and the compass necklace looped around her neck. She held her pencil, sketching lines lightly, the limestone arch of Cathedral Cove slowly taking shape on the page. A well of emotions stirred as she drew; she was hopeful she would see Max in a few short hours, nervous that if this worked, if this really worked, then she had some supernatural control over her dreams.

She lost track of time as she sketched, lost in the New Zealand landscape on the paper. There was a light tap on the door.

She slipped the compass underneath the collar of her shirt.

"Come in," she said, lifting her head.

Julie peeked her head inside Cora's room, and Cora saw her dad in the hallway behind her.

"How are things going in here?" her mom asked, a smile on her face.

"Good," Cora replied. She stretched her legs and raised her arms over her head. Her muscles still ached from her nightly adventures.

"Can we come in?" Julie asked, tentatively.

Cora nodded and folded her knees back in towards her chest, wrapping her arms around her bent legs.

Her mom smiled again as they came in and sat on the floor next to her. Her dad grunted as he crouched to the floor. He crossed his legs before exclaiming, "I'm too old to sit like this," and bent his knees, so his arms draped over them. His hands were clasped together in front of him.

"Cora, we want to see how you're doing." He cleared his throat. "I know you and Max were close, really close. And we just wanted to check in, see how you're doing with everything."

"Oh, well, yeah. I mean, I miss him a lot," Cora was caught off guard and the tears came like a tsunami. "I just miss him a lot." She was crying now, her shoulders shaking.

"I know, honey," her mom said, wiping her own tear-streaked face. "I know. I miss him too, so much." They sat, arms and legs tangled in one tear-filled mess. Her dad sat with his head dipped, slowly rubbing his eyes with one hand.

"Would you want to talk to someone? I don't know, like a therapist or something?" her dad asked. "Just to help sort out feelings and stuff?"

"Not really," Cora said, sniffling.

Her dad nodded slowly. "Well, if that changes, please, please let us know. And we'll talk to Reagan," he said, gesturing with his hands to the room next door. "Everyone deals with sadness differently, but she can't lash out at you. It's not fair."

"It's okay. I think Reagan is having a harder time than we realize. I could probably be more kind," Cora said, reflecting Max's advice. "I'll never, ever regret being kind, even if she isn't kind back."

Her parents sat, mouths slightly open, silent for a few seconds before responding. "Yeah, uh, yeah, you can't argue that," her dad stuttered. "Well, can we do anything to help?" Ned was a fixer. He liked to solve problems and liked things to be linear and exact. It was probably why he liked tinkering in the garage, and why he was so successful as an accountant. Follow the instructions, follow the rules and everything will be right again. Follow the tax laws, follow the mathematical formulas, and the numbers line up. Cora figured he was desperate to fix this, too.

"I think what your dad is trying to say is that we're here for you, in any way you need. If you want to talk to us, we're here. If you want to talk to a professional, we can arrange that." She stroked Cora's hair. "We're all going to feel sad for a while and that's normal. We just want you to know that we are here. Always. No matter what."

Cora nodded and smiled. "Thanks," she said.

Her mom gave her a tight squeeze, and the cold metal of the compass pressed into her chest. Her dad lifted the sketchpad and looked carefully at the drawing of Cathedral Cove.

"Is this your New Zealand project?"

Cora nodded. "It's a place called Cathedral Cove. There's a giant arch and the water comes through it. It's right on the beach."

"It looks awesome," he said, handing her the sketchpad. "You're so good at drawing."

Cora picked up her pencil, anxious to start sketching again. Sensing her readiness, her parents raised themselves off the carpet.

"We'll let you get back to sketching," her mom said. "I'm excited to see it when it's done."

"I might say goodnight now," Cora said, feigning a yawn. "I'm going to draw a few more minutes and then go to bed."

Her mom and dad nodded. "Good night, sweetie," they said, kissing her cheek. Cora couldn't wait for the door to close behind them before she resumed sketching.

She wasn't sure how long she drew, but her eyelids drooped like two heavy curtains. She flopped onto her bed, propped on her elbows, and compared her sketch to the printed pages lying on the floor. She doodled a little sketch in the corner of a glowworm cave before succumbing to sleep.

Chapter 24

SOMETHING WARM PRESSED AGAINST Cora's face. She pushed herself up and brushed tiny granules of fine sand from her hands. She smiled and a thrill filled her. Cora still wasn't entirely sure how this worked, or what sort of realm she was really in, but it seemed to have a pattern. Maybe the magic was in the sketchpad. She knew Max was here somewhere, and she wanted to find him as soon as possible.

She stood and tucked the compass necklace underneath her shirt. She walked to the edge of the beach, saw the white frothing waves from the sea licking the sand beneath her feet. Green shrubs peppered the hills surrounding the cove, the horizon spanning as far as her eyes could see. She looked up, taking in the gigantic rock cavern. The cathedral-shaped arch gave the entire beach a feeling of grandeur.

"Pretty spectacular, huh?" Max's voice was behind her.

"How did you get here?" Her heart leaping at the sight of Max.

"How did you?" he retorted, his eyes twinkling. He didn't give her time to answer. "This place... is incredible."

Max walked to the edge of the water and turned his head slowly from side to side, breathing it all in.

"You don't realize how beautiful the world really is," he said. "How vast it is, how much there is to see."

His eyes were trained on the horizon, his gaze far off. "When you're in it, you're kind of stuck in your own little world, stuck inside your own bubble. It's hard to see your way out sometimes." He was quiet for a moment. "But there's a whole world, Cora. When your world feels small, don't forget to look outside yourself."

He looked at her, his eyes and smile bright.

"So, let's go see it," she said, matching his smile. When she was with Max, she was more confident, surer of herself. She wished she could feel this way at school, at home.

Max raised his eyebrows, surprised at her tenacity. "Let's go then!"

They turned, their feet sinking lightly in the damp sand. They followed a short set of stairs, and then a sandy trail upward, winding along the coastline. Cora looked out to see turquoise waters and golden beaches.

"So, when are you going to try out for the volleyball team?" Max interrupted her thoughts.

"How did you know about that?" Heat rose to Cora's cheeks, embarrassment that she had entertained the idea.

Max tapped his temple and gave her a sly smile. "I know a lot of things."

"I don't think I'm going to do it," she said softly, looking down at her feet. "I probably wouldn't even make it."

"Who cares if you don't make it?" Max said. "You've already not made the team. Why don't you at least try, see what you've got? The worst that could happen is you don't make the team, and that's exactly where you are now."

"No, the worst that could happen is that someone hits me in the face with a ball and I get a bloody nose and make a mess on the gym floor and embarrass myself."

Max laughed and then stopped himself quickly. "Oh, you're serious, that's a serious concern. Okay. Well, if that happens, if that is the worst thing that could happen, then what would you do?"

"Well, it would be embarrassing to go back to school." she said. "Everyone would talk and laugh about it."

"Maybe," Max nodded. "Maybe not, though. What makes you think people care?"

Cora was quiet. Her face was hot. She thought of the stares, the whispered conversations behind hands as she walked by.

"I'm just saying that most people aren't as concerned with others as you think they are," Max said. "Especially in middle school. Everyone else is just like you. Worried about what other people think. They don't care or even notice what you're doing. Plus... what if you actually made the team? That'd be awesome."

"You don't get it. I'm not like you and Reagan, Max," Cora shook her head. "You guys are good at sports and stuff. I'm not. I'm..." She could barely say it. "Awkward," she said finally, so quietly she wasn't even sure Max could hear.

"Awkward?" he repeated, making sure he heard her correctly. "Who isn't awkward at times? I know I am."

Unexpected tears sprang to Cora's eyes. Max was her champion; he always had been. She missed his support, missed his encouragement. Her mom and dad were always supportive, and always encouraged her, but they were her parents, and their support seemed obligatory at times. Max didn't have to believe in her, yet he did.

"I don't know," she said quietly. They had reached a wide, vacant parking lot.

"I do, Cora. I do know," he said, emphatically. "And I know that you cannot let what one person said about you one time define you."

She wondered how he knew about the conversation between Reagan and her friend.

"It's not just that, though. I mean, yeah, Reagan's friend did say that, and it has stuck with me, but it is true." Her voice cracked with emotion. "I told you, I'm not like you and Reagan. You guys are good at everything you try, you're popular, you have tons of friends. I have one friend, I'm not popular, and I'm not good at anything."

Max let the silence hang between them, and Cora wondered if he finally saw her for what she really was.

"Cora, the world needs you to be who you are," he said. "Who you really are. So maybe you aren't the most athletic person ever, but you have a lot else going for you. There will be plenty of people to tell you that you are too shy, or too awkward, or too whatever, but that's just them being insecure about themselves. Don't forget that."

She kept her eyes focused on the empty parking lot. *Don't cry, don't cry, don't cry.* Max's confidence in her made her feel like an imposter. Like he saw some grand version of herself, when she knew the real counterfeit version.

Max surveyed the parking lot. As if he could sense her growing discomfort, he graciously changed the subject.

"Now what?" he asked.

Cora eyed two bikes, perched against a faded, wooden sign.

"Want to take a ride?" she asked.

Max raised his eyebrows, clearly surprised by her comment. She surprised herself, too. Cora normally followed all of the rules, but the risk was worth spending more time with Max.

"Let's do it," Max said. He was already walking towards the bikes.

Cora jogged to catch up with him, steadying herself with one leg and swinging her other leg over the bike, finding the pedals with her feet. They rode, side by side, following a winding road. A warm breeze rustled through Cora's hair, sending it flowing wildly around her. They rode in silence, absorbing the scenery around them. Cora watched Max as she rode. She saw the smile creep onto his face, watched his eyes behold all the glory of his dream destination. A twinge of guilt pulled at her insides, having this surreal moment with Max when the rest of her family was in such pain.

They sped along the road, riding alongside the lush green hills.

"Check out the arch," Max said, steering the bike with one hand and using the other to point out the giant limestone arch on the side of the road. He stopped at a pull-off spot on the side of the road, peering over the ledge.

He looked at Cora, excitement dancing in his eyes. Cora's stomach dropped as she got closer, realizing the plunge to the beach below. It made her sick to look that far down.

Max spotted a well-worn trail down. "What do you think?" He hitched his thumb behind him, pointing out the trail to Cora.

They leapt from their bikes, their feet pounding down the dirt path. It was steep, but short, and before long they were at the opening of a cave. Cora swallowed the growing lump in her throat as Max craned his neck forward, trying to see inside. Cora took a step backwards, physically distancing herself. She didn't like total darkness, she didn't like closed spaces, and she definitely didn't like being in an unfamiliar place that was also totally dark and closed in. Claustrophobia was already setting in.

"I'm not going in there," she shook her head vehemently.

"Why not?" Max asked. His eyebrows were knit together, his face twisted in confusion.

"Who knows what's in there! It could be dangerous!"

"But it could be amazing, too," he countered.

She stepped closer to the cavernous hole, her eyes straining to see inside. She blinked, waiting for her eyes to adjust to the darkness, trying to grasp onto some variance in the darkness, a shadow, a glimmer of light, but it was an endless cloak of black.

"I'm not going in there," she repeated resolutely.

"Okay, that's fine. I'm not going to force you," Max said. "But sometimes, the things that scare us the most are the most rewarding. It just takes stepping into the darkness a little bit before you see the light."

"But it doesn't look like there is any light in there at all," Cora protested. "And there's water. I'm not walking in that water in the dark."

Max pointed at something behind her, and when Cora turned around, she saw two inflated black innertubes. Cora's mouth dropped at the sight of them.

"Looks like we don't have to walk. We can ride." Max smiled. His eyes were shining, a wide grin plastered on his face.

"Have those always been there?" she asked.

Max shrugged. "I don't know. I didn't notice them before. But they're here now!" He clapped his hands together.

He walked past her, pushed his hands down on the innertubes to check the inflation.

"These will be just right," he said, satisfied. "If you change your mind, that is."

Cora looked from Max back to the cave. The thought of sitting in an inner tube in a total darkness, surrounded by water, made her palms sweat. She swallowed the lump in her throat. *The longer you wait, the bigger it gets.*

"Let's do it," she said quickly, before she could change her mind.

Max smiled and handed her an inner tube. They waded into the water.

"It's just like the ladder," Max said, beside her. "Just take the next step forward. Don't worry about the other stuff right now."

She lunged onto her innertube, propelling herself forward and into the dark. The silence in the cave was unnerving. Inky blackness surrounded her.

She swiveled her head behind her looking for Max, but she only saw darkness.

"Max?" she called timidly. Her voice echoed, bouncing off the walls and coming back at her from all directions.

"I think I'm behind you. This is awesome." His voice was breathless and excited.

Her inner tube slowed. She tried bouncing, trying to inch her tube forward. The water around her sloshed against the rubber, but her tube stayed put.

"Max? Are you still moving?" She asked into the darkness.

"Yes, aren't you?" Max asked with a laugh. "Are you using your hands?"

Cora hesitated. No, she definitely wasn't using her hands as paddles. She cringed at the thought of putting her hands in the murky water. Max understood her silence as an answer.

"I think you're going to have to use your hands as paddles," Max said. His voice was right next to her.

"No. I don't want to. I can't."

"Then we're probably not going to make it much further," Max said. He was calm, nonchalant. His disembodied voice was more distant now, floating further into the shadowy cave. She thought about how the darkness had just swallowed him up, and she shuddered.

"Where are you?" she asked timidly. The dark cave seemed to swallow her up.

"I'm not that far in front of you," he said. "I'm stopped, and I won't go any further without you."

Cora knew the toes of her shoes had been dragging lightly in the water, but since she couldn't feel the water on her skin, she could pretend like it wasn't happening. Using her hands as paddles was different. She would feel the water, and her skin would feel anything below the surface. She winced at the thought.

Her fleeting moment of bravado from earlier was gone. She tried talking herself into it. *Just dip one finger,* she told herself. She tried waiting.

"Cora? You okay?" Max called from the darkness ahead.

"I want to go back out," Cora replied, her voice high and uneven. "I can't—I can't put my hands in the water. I'm too scared."

"The longer you wait, the bigger it gets," Max reminded her. His voice was getting closer, and Cora knew he was coming back for her.

"But it's scary," she countered.

Max was quiet for a moment before responding.

"It is scary for sure," he said. And Cora was dismayed that he didn't immediately assuage her fears. "But your fear won't fade until you actually take a step toward the big, scary thing. Until you do something about it."

"It will if I just leave the cave," Cora said.

"You'll still have to paddle out," Max said patiently. "Your tube is totally stopped, so you have to use your hands no matter what."

Cora's stomach tightened. She hadn't thought about that.

"It's totally up to you, Cor. I'll follow you wherever you go," Max said, a familiar kindness in his voice. "All it takes is one second," Max said, his voice right next to her now. "One second of being really, incredibly brave. Once you get going, you see it's not so scary after all."

One second and the decision to be brave. To plunge her hands into the black water.

"It's more than a few seconds, Max." Cora was stalling.

"Once you take that first step, once you put your hands in the water, you've already tackled the hardest part."

Cora inhaled deeply, and on the exhale pushed her hands deep into the water. It was cool, and Cora tried to picture herself in a clear, light swimming pool.

Max cheered loudly. The reverberating echo startled both of them. "That was awesome, Cora!" His enthusiasm was contagious, and Cora smiled to herself in the darkness.

"I couldn't have done that without you," Cora said.

"I didn't do anything," Max said. "That was all you. You're the one who decided to be brave. You're the one who had the courage to put your hands in the water."

She was paddling comfortably now, propelling herself forward and circling back, the water splashing gently against her tube.

"I know, but you believed in me. You knew I could do it," she said. Immense gratitude for Max, for his confidence in her filled her soul. "So, are we going to see what this cave is all about or what?"

"Lead the way!" Max said.

She paddled deeper into the darkness. Sometimes, she realized, overcoming one small fear gives you enough confidence to keep going, even when there are more right in front of you.

As she paddled, Cora was surprised to see a faint blue light in the distance. She could hear Max close by, light splashes made by his hands.

"How's Reagan doing?" Max asked, quietly from somewhere beside her.

"I don't know. She just hangs out in her room all the time, and she doesn't hardly ever come out. I barely see her," Cora said. "And when she does talk to me, she isn't very nice, so I'm okay with not seeing her much."

"Did you try giving her that bracelet?"

Guilt rose in Cora's throat. Not only had she not given her the bracelet, but she had decided not to.

"Try it," Max said. "When have you ever known Reagan to stay in her room? Never. I think she's struggling more than anyone realizes."

"We're all struggling, Max," Cora said, relieved the cloak of darkness surrounding them hid the emotion on her face. "It's not the same without you."

"I know it's hard for everyone," he said finally, his voice thick with emotion. "I know that. But Cora, you guys have to know that I'm okay. You have to know that I'm alive and doing more work, just in a different way than you guys."

"What kind of work?" Cora asked.

"I can't really explain it," Max said. "But you have to know that. You have to tell Mom and Dad and Reagan that even though I'm not with you guys, even though I'm gone, I'm okay."

Cora was silent. The darkness seemed to bolster her confidence, and Cora asked the question she had been wondering since that first day in the forest.

"How am I seeing you? These feel like dreams, but then I wake up and I'm soaking wet with sand everywhere. So, then it doesn't feel like a dream."

"I don't know," Max said, thoughtfully. "Maybe one day we'll figure it out."

They paddled in the darkness, each lost in their own thoughts.

"Cora," Max said softly. "You can be the one who brings everyone together now. Maybe it was me before, but it needs to be you now."

Cora shook her head automatically before remembering Max couldn't see it. One of the hardest parts of her grief was not only that she desperately missed Max, but it was also the debris his death left in its wake; she not only lost her brother, but she was grieving the loss of her family, too. Grief was like that. Drop an enormous boulder in a lake and the initial drop is shattering and shocking, but the wake is devastating in a different, catastrophic way.

"I don't even know where to start," Cora said, quietly.

"Love her, Cora. Love is the most powerful force in the world," Max replied.

Cora was quiet. Deep down, she did love Reagan. She just didn't like her very much, which made it hard to show her love.

"Whoa," Cora said breathlessly. Teal lights twinkled in a starry wonderland above them. It was everything Cora imagined it would be. Magical and ethereal, a galaxy of tiny, living lights.

"This is awesome." Max punctuated each word.

Cora was awestruck. The glow worms illuminated the cave enough that Cora saw Max looking up in wonder. The luminescent glow worms stretched as far as she could see, trailing down the narrow cave. They were silent, taking in the majesty above them. She craned her neck, her eyes scanning the vast, gleaming lights above her.

"Can you believe this?" Max asked. He was ahead of her, and his voice echoed around her.

"No," Cora said quietly.

"Cora, this..." Max was gesturing with his hand toward the cave ceiling, indicating the illuminated lights. "This is what's on the other side of fear. Something bigger and better and indescribable. But it takes courage and bravery, and it takes going through some scary stuff to get there sometimes. But something extraordinary is almost always on the other side."

He was closer to her now, the glow worms casting a dim blue light on his face. Cora looked from Max to the spectacular sky above, glittering with possibilities. They sat, under the shimmering glow worms for a long time, each absorbed in their own thoughts.

Cora shivered. She was getting cold, and her arms were still sore from climbing that waterfall. Her midnight adventures left her severely lacking sleep.

"Pretty cool, Cor," Max said. He paddled aimlessly, the water making a soft lapping against his tube.

"Mmm hmm," Cora agreed. She was getting sleepy.

Maybe she could rest her head for just a minute. She crooked her elbow into a makeshift pillow. The muscles in her body softened, melting into the tube. She fought to keep her eyes open, but the darkness around her lulled her to sleep.

"Cora!" She jolted at the sound of Max's voice.

Suddenly she flipped off her tube, landing upside down in the water. She thrashed recklessly, unsure of what to do. The sudden immersion in the water took her breath away, and her inner tube was nowhere in sight. She had drifted away from the luminescent glow worms and was now surrounded by darkness. She flailed in the water, trying to stay afloat and trying to keep her panic at bay as she circled her arms in front of her, searching blindly for her innertube. *Where w Max?* she wondered. Something smooth and elastic grazed her fngertips, but the tube dipped beyond her reach before she could grasp it. Panic rose into her throat and she let out a guttural yell, a combination of terror and frustration.

"Cora!" Max yelled again.

"I'm here!" Cora yelled. The reverberating echo made it impossible to determine where Max was, and she wondered if her voice was doing the same thing to him.

"Are you in the water?"

"I can't find my tube!" Cora wailed.

"I'll try to find you!" Max called from the distance.

"Okay, Cora," she said aloud to herself. She was treading water now, her feet and hands circling, keeping her afloat. "Take a breath and focus." She forced herself to take a breath. "Now, find your tube."

Talking herself through the steps was working; she was more self-assured, more confident in what she needed to do. She stretched her arms in front of her, blindly reaching for her inner tube. She kicked her feet, propelling her forward a few feet. With every kick, Cora was more and more defeated. She was cold and tired. Suddenly, her fingers grazed something smooth above the water. Her tube! With a surge of energy, Cora heaved herself from the water, hooking one arm over the top of the tube, holding it with her elbow. She breathed heavily. She had exerted nearly all of her energy in the cave, and she was exhausted. She wasn't even sure she could muster the strength to climb atop the tube. She took a deep breath. Ready... go. She used her arm anchoring the tube to pull herself on top, but the tube shot away from her.

Cora choked on mouthful of water. She grasped for the rubber tube again, keeping it within her reach. She couldn't search for that tube in the dark again; she didn't have the physical stamina. She hooked it again with her other arm this time and tried again. She flopped her body on the tube, but the uneven weight tipped her into the water again. Cora whimpered, frustrated, defeated and unsure of what else to do.

Try again, she told herself. She hooked her arm again and pulled herself onto the top of the tube. The tube rocked on the water but stayed upright. The compass! She needed to make sure it was still on the necklace. Blindly,

Cora's fingers found the compass on her neck, and closed around the golden globe.

Chapter 25

HER CLOTHES WERE SOAKED, leaving a wet little puddle on her sheets. She longed for a hot shower to warm her bones, but she knew Reagan was probably waiting up for her to do just that. Her arms ached and her body was fatigued in a way she'd never felt before. She peeled her wet clothes off, layer by layer, throwing them in her laundry hamper. She put on her favorite pair of pajamas and buried herself under her blankets. She shivered and wrapped herself in a ball. Her breathing turned rhythmic, and she found, again, she couldn't keep her eyelids open.

As she fell asleep, she wondered where Max had gone. Why had he left her to fend for herself when she needed him most?

❖

Reagan sat in her bed, her back propped against pillows. Her room was dark, except for the small glowing screen in front of her. She hit the small blue triangle again, replaying a voice message, a call she had ignored days ago from Coach Sadler.

"Uh, hey, Reagan, it's Coach Sadler. I just wanted to talk to you and see where your head's at..." He paused. "Listen, the coach at Buckhead called. He said he hasn't been able to reach you and he's getting a little concerned."

Reagan rolled her eyes in the dark. There was that word again. Concerned. Everyone was concerned. His voice continued, tinny through the speaker.

"Anyway, just seeing if you wanted to come in sometime this week and kick the ball around or just talk or whatever. I'd hate to see you lose your scholarship."

And there it was, the reason for his call. The Buckhead coach wasn't concerned about her well-being. He was concerned about his upcoming soccer season. *He should be concerned,* Reagan thought. *Because I couldn't care less if I lost that scholarship.*

She clicked the red garbage can icon and watched as the voicemail, the message filled with so much concern, slid into an electronic garbage can.

She sighed and set her phone down next to her, thinking about how easy it was to delete that voicemail, how easily it slipped into a digital dumpster, and she could pretend it never existed. Sometimes, she wished she could just slip away. Soccer and friendships and boyfriends and school had ceased to bring her any joy or excitement. Sometimes, she just wanted to slip into oblivion.

Reagan sighed again, bored. Her circadian rhythms were off, causing her to stay awake all night and sleep during the bright, daytime hours. *Maybe it's a coping mechanism,* she thought. *If I'm asleep during the day, when everyone else is awake, I don't have to see or talk to anyone. And Cora won't bother me.* The thought of Cora made Reagan's eyes widen with excitement. She threw the covers off and crept out of bed. She cracked her door open and saw Cora's light was off. On quiet feet she tiptoed down the hallway and gently opened Cora's door, peering inside. A nightlight glowed in the corner of the room and Reagan rolled her eyes again. Her little sister was such a baby. Cora was buried under a pile of blankets, breathing steadily. Reagan closed the door.

She looked down the hall, noticed Max's door just past Cora's. Positioned at the end of the hall, it was easy to avoid. She had only been in his room once since he died, when her mom was ransacking his drawers and closet, searching desperately for his compass.

She wasn't sure if it was boredom or something else that pulled her to his room, but before she realized it, she was at his door. The doorknob was cold under her hand as she turned it slowly. She flicked a switch and light poured from the ceiling. Reagan was surprised everything had been put back where it belonged, as if Max was just gone for the night. His bed was neatly made, his blue sheets just barely visible.

Trophies and awards were perched on shelves, punctuated by framed pictures of family and friends. A signed baseball from one of his favorite professional players sat amidst items.

Many days, Reagan wished it was her that was gone. Max was too good, he had too much to offer. He was kind and happy and outgoing, he was talented and smart. She pulled a picture from the shelf—Max's recreational basketball team. He stood in the middle, cradling a ball in both hands. Reagan thought of how fitting it was that he stood in the center, always in the middle, always the one to bring people together. Like their family.

The picture in her hands was old. Max had grown at least one foot since the picture had been taken, but his eyes were the same. Deep brown eyes stared into hers, and a sense of sadness washed over her.

Maybe it was being back in his space, surrounded by his things. She thought of that night when her mom had torn through Max's room. Reagan had never seen her mom in such a frantic state, and it unnerved her. She had been near manic, her eyes wild and red as she flung open drawers and flipping over every sheet of paper on his desk. She turned pants inside out, searched jacket pockets. Reagan thought about that, and for the first time in she didn't know how long, thought of how her mom and dad must feel.

The thought weakened her knees, and she sat on the side of his bed, buried her face in her hands, and cried. She didn't know how long she sat on his bed, crying into her hands, but when she was done, she had a new resolve: find Max's compass. It would be her token, her peace offering, her olive branch to her broken parents.

Chapter 26

CORA WINCED WHEN SHE woke up. Her arms were sore and her shoulders ached with stiff muscles. She got out of bed, preemptively turned her alarm off, and opened her bedroom door. Downstairs, bowls clattered and dishes clinked in the sink. Reagan's door was closed. Cora crept by Reagan's door, slinking down the stairs.

"Morning, Mom," she chirped as she entered the kitchen. Her mom's back was to her, a bowl in hand whisking a thick, white batter. Cora saw her jump a little at the sudden noise, but she turned and smiled brightly.

"Morning, sweetie! I didn't expect you to be up yet," she said, still whisking. The hot scent of the griddle heating up reached her nose.

"Mom, volleyball tryouts are coming up, and I want to go." Cora said abruptly.

Her mom paused the whisk and blinked in surprise.

"Oh, okay! That's a great idea, honey," she said, nodding. "I didn't know you were interested in volleyball."

Cora shrugged. "I don't know if I'll like it, but I want to try."

"When are they? What do you need for that?" She set the bowl on the counter, listening intently.

"I don't know what I need, and I think they're soon." Cora shrugged. "I saw a poster at school."

"Okay. We can figure it out. Check the poster today and see when the tryouts are." She smiled at Cora and resumed her whisking. "I'm proud of you for trying something new."

"Thanks, Mom." Cora swiveled on the barstool and hopped off. "I'm going to hurry and get ready."

Cora hurried up the stairs. A flurry of excitement filled her. She didn't know a thing about volleyball, but she yearned to be part of something bigger, part of a team. Above all else, she wanted to feel like she belonged somewhere.

Chapter 27

CORA WALKED THROUGH THE automatic glass doors of her school. Groups of friends were clustered together, and Cora wondered what it would be like to have more than one friend, to walk into the school and look for familiar faces. Mia was, and always would be, her best friend, there was no doubting that. Cora just wished they had other friends, so when one of them was sick or taking a test during lunch, the other didn't have to sit by themselves.

She walked to her locker, passing the volleyball tryout sign. Tomorrow afternoon at three o'clock. It didn't specify equipment needed and gave the gym teacher's name for any questions. Cora was suddenly second guessing her decision, but remembered Max's advice.

You've already not made the team. What's the worst that could happen?

At her locker, she deposited her books and notebook, then pulled out her math book and supplies. Math was Cora's least favorite subject. It was only bearable because Mia was in her class and the two were always partners.

Cora walked to Mia's locker, searching for her friend. No Mia. She scanned the crowd for Mia's crop of curly brown hair. Nothing. Worried people would see her standing with no one to talk to, Cora knelt, pretending to tie her shoes. Still no sign of Mia.

The hallway traffic was dwindling, and Cora didn't want to be late for class. She walked the short distance from Mia's locker to her math class and noticed that the seat next to her was empty. *Mia must be gone today*, she thought, a pit growing in her stomach. Cora said a silent prayer that today wouldn't be a partner day.

She had time to sit in her desk and lay out her math supplies before the bell rang.

"Okay, let's get started a little early," her teacher said, ignoring the chatter in the classroom. "We have a lot to cover today." She scanned the classroom, quickly making note of any absences.

"Looks like we're missing Mia," she said. "And Marcus." She set her notebook down on her desk and made her way to the front of the classroom. "Today we're going to be using our protractors, so I sure hope everyone brought theirs."

"Mrs. Courtney, I don't have my protractor today," someone from across the room said.

"You can borrow mine after I'm done with the demonstration, Miles," she replied, tucking her bob-length hair behind her ears. "But make sure you give it back to me at the end of class."

"Today we're going to use these to learn how to draw angles." She held up the clear plastic piece, shaped like a half circle. Her hair bounced as she looked around the room. "Remember last class how we talked about acute, right, and obtuse angles?"

The class watched quietly.

"This isn't a rhetorical question," Mrs. Courtney said, her thin lips pursed. "Your reactions tell me no one remembers." She paused, and a few heads nodded.

"Okay, quick recap," she sighed. "Acute angles are small, less than ninety degrees. Right angles are ninety degrees exactly, and obtuse angles are greater than ninety degrees. Got it?"

More heads nodded. Cora furiously scribbled notes in her notebook.

She turned and walked to the whiteboard, grabbing a black dry erase marker. She demonstrated drawing an angle quickly. Cora's mind spun. She was confused already.

"Make sense?" she asked, turning back to face the whiteboard. "Let's try another one. This time, we're going to draw an acute fifty-degree angle."

She turned around to make sure everyone was following along. "Make sense so far? Does anyone have any questions?"

The class stared mutely.

"I'll take silence as confirmation that there are no questions, so we'll keep moving." At the whiteboard, Mrs. Courtney worked through different angles, drawing lines and holding the protractor against the board. Occasionally she turned to the class, evaluating their blank faces.

She turned to face the class again. "Pretty straightforward, yeah?" She looked at their blank faces. Cora glanced furtively around her, trying to read facial expressions. Was anyone as lost as she was? Her head was swimming, a jumble of numbers and degrees and things that didn't make sense to her.

Mrs. Courtney pulled a stack of papers from her desk and handed them to the end of the U shape arrangement of desks. "Take one and pass it down, please," she said. "We're going to partner up and practice drawing different types of angles. Tyler. You and Cora can partner up today, since you're both missing your usual partners."

Tyler's eyes darted to his friends, who smirked at him and shrugged. He looked at Cora and she blushed, heat climbing up her neck and onto her cheeks. People around her shuffled to their partners or turned in their seats. She avoided Tyler's eyes, too embarrassed to make eye contact.

"Do you want me to come over there?" he asked.

"Uh, yeah, no, I can come...whatever is fine," she stuttered. *Off to a great start,* she thought.

Tyler stood from his chair and trudged to the empty desk next to her. He slid into the chair and tapped his pencil, eraser-side down on the desk.

"What are we supposed to do?" he asked, looking at his instructions.

"I think we're just supposed to practice drawing some angles," Cora said. Her cheeks blazed and she tried to avoid all eye contact with Tyler. She pulled her paper closer to her, pretending to re-read the instructions. "So, it looks like we're supposed to draw a forty-five-degree angle, a seventy-degree angle, and a one hundred and forty-degree angle first."

She and Tyler worked silently, drawing lines and arrows, labeling angles. Cora understood the acute angles, but paused when she got to the third obtuse one.

She made her ray, set her mark, and drew her angle. Tyler watched her intently.

"I think your ray needs to go the other way," he said. "That's what Mrs. Courtney was saying." He lined up his protractor, and finished his one hundred and forty-degree angle.

"Oh, yeah, you're right," Cora said. She turned her pencil around and erased furiously, ripping her paper. She was embarrassed, sweat prickling on her hairline.

Tyler remained silent next to her. Somehow his silence intensified her embarrassment.

She straightened her paper and drew her ray, adding the arrow to the other side. She found the mark and connected her lines, but it didn't look right. She stole a sneaky glance at Tyler's paper. His angle was much wider. She quickly erased her mistake, but Tyler noticed.

"Go to the other mark." He tapped his protractor to show her where.

Tyler mouthed something to his friends across the room, and tears of embarrassment sprang to her eyes. She tried to wipe them away discreetly. The only thing that could be worse about this situation was if Tyler saw her crying over geometry.

She made her mark, connected her lines, and labeled her angle correctly.

"Sorry," she said, quietly, and if Tyler heard her, he didn't acknowledge it.

"Now we have to do a two hundred and fifty-degree reflex angle." He looked at the board. "Wait. That's the one Mrs. Courtney already did, so we can just copy what's on the board." He looked from the board to this paper, copying what Mrs. Courtney had already solved. When he was done, he grabbed his paper and left quickly, without saying a word to Cora.

Cora kept her eyes trained on the whiteboard and her paper. She couldn't make eye contact with Tyler, or with his friends, or with anyone else.

The bell blared. As quickly as possible, Cora grabbed her notebooks and supplies, not even bothering to put her protractor in her pencil case. She held back tears the entire walk to the bathroom.

Once inside, she stood in front of the mirror, staring at her reflection. Splotchy red patches covered her ivory skin, and frizzy wisps of copper hair strayed from her hairline. She replayed Tyler and his friends laughing and exchanging glances, and tears filled her eyes again. A recurring thought filled her mind. *If I looked like Reagan,* she thought, *Tyler would be excited to partner with me.* That thought ran through her head in a continuous, circular loop. Reagan was the pretty one, Max had been the fun one, and she was just Cora, the awkward one. The outsider with red hair and knobby knees.

She thought of Max, and more tears filled her eyes. Max would know just what to say to her to make her feel better. She stayed in the bathroom long enough for her face to return to its normal light pink hue, deliberating what to do. The bell hadn't rung signaling the beginning of the next class, but it would soon. Cora knew she would be late if she didn't hurry. But if she waited until the hallway was empty, no one could stare at her. She decided to take the tardy.

The rest of the day passed in a blurry haze, marred by Cora's embarrassment in first period math. Cora cringed when the bell sounded for lunch. She hated when Mia was gone because it meant she had to eat by herself.

She sat at a corner table, nibbling her peanut butter sandwich quickly. Lunch was the halfway point in the day, so she had two classes left. Her last class of the day, science, was with Tyler. She shuddered at the thought of facing him again. She gathered the remnants of her lunch and dumped them in the trash can, glancing at the clock in the cafeteria. Seventeen minutes of lunchtime left, and she was unsure what to do to fill her time. She walked to her locker and retrieved her sketchpad and pencil. There was a small alcove, sequestered away from the cafeteria where she could draw, and no one would really see she was alone, without any friends.

She sat, her back against the brick wall, her knees bent and her sketchpad propped against her legs. She looked around, searching for inspiration. Directly in front of her she saw a picture of a desert. Contoured dunes emerged from rippled, windswept sand. The desert scene seemed to stretch on for miles past the picture, an endless sea of undulating copper sand. It looked like a foreign planet. She touched her pencil to the paper, making swift, light lines. Holding the sketchpad out in front of her, she examined her work. It wasn't perfect, but she could definitely see the resemblance. As she sketched, time slipped away from her. She forgot about the students eating lunch behind her, forgot she was sitting all alone in the hallway until a voice interrupted her thoughts.

"Hey." The voice was familiar.

Cora looked up and let out a small gasp. Tyler.

"Hey," she replied, averting her eyes to her sketchpad.

"You left your protractor in Mrs. Courtney's class," he said, motioning to the classroom with his thumb.

"Thanks," Cora mumbled. She peeked from her sketchpad to see Tyler was still standing there. "I'll get it after lunch," she said without looking up.

She could see his feet, still planted. Why wouldn't he just leave?

"Yeah, cool." His feet shuffled awkwardly, but he wasn't walking away. She looked up.

"Did you eat out here?" he asked, looking around for signs of her lunch.

Cora shook her head, heat rushing to her cheeks. "No, I already ate. I wanted to finish some work for art class," she lied, hoping he wouldn't ask when she had art, because it wasn't one of her electives this semester.

"Oh, cool." He nodded.

Cora couldn't comprehend why he was still standing there in front of her, talking to her. Tyler was one of the most popular boys in her grade. He was handsome, with wavy, sandy-brown hair and olive skin. He had straight white teeth, without the help of braces. Tyler looked down at his feet.

"I'm sorry about what happened to your brother," he said finally, still looking at his feet. "My older brother was in the same grade, and... Sorry."

Cora recoiled slightly. She didn't know Tyler had a brother, let alone a brother in the same grade as Max.

She scrambled to find something to say. It was a blended wave of surprise and sadness that washed over her, leaving her speechless.

Tyler took her silence as his exit.

"Anyway. See you around." He turned and walked away, leaving Cora in a stunned silence.

"Bye," she said quietly, though she was sure he couldn't hear her.

The bell rang, and Cora stood, clutching her sketchpad tightly. She walked closer to the picture, trying to memorize the details.

"Wahiba Sands," she said, reading the words from the bottom right corner of the picture. "Wahiba Sands."

She walked to her locker and pulled out her English notebook and the book they were reading as a class. English was another class she loved, mostly because for a portion of every period, they were allowed to read anything they wanted. Cora loved being able to escape into another story. After English was her last class, science. Her stomach tightened involuntarily at the thought of facing Tyler again.

English passed too quickly for Cora. She wanted to stay in the warm cocoon of her book, where she could burrow, far away from herself, from her looming science class.

She exchanged notebooks and textbooks in her locker, hurrying to her science class. She slid into her desk, one of the first students in the classroom. She opened her notebook, pretending to be studying intently, reviewing notes from the last class.

She kept her eyes low as students filed in, the classroom quickly filling. Her eyes were focused on her notebook in front of her. She turned a page so anyone watching might think she was actually reading the words in front of her.

The bell rang, and her teacher, Mr. Finley, approached the front of the classroom.

"Today we're covering everyone's favorite topic." He paused for dramatic effect. "Photosynthesis!" He raised his hands in mock celebration.

Cora's eyes veered slightly, drifting over the classroom. Tyler must have sensed her gaze, because he turned to look at her just as she looked at him, nodding his head slightly and giving her a small smile.

She smiled in return and quickly averted her gaze. Her stomach flipped.

Mr. Finley drew a sunflower, complete with roots nestled below ground, and leaves sprouting from the stem. He drew symbols on the whiteboard, gesturing with his hands to show how the process worked. Cora tried to listen, but the sequence of embarrassing moments earlier haunted her. She winced when she remembered how awkward she had been. If Tyler didn't think she was totally weird after the math incident, he did after their interaction in the hallway. She shook her head, trying to dislodge the memory from her brain.

"So, the sun is providing energy for the plants," Mr. Finley said as Cora managed to direct her attention back to science class. The bell rang. Cora gathered her books and stood from her desk, dodging everyone and making a beeline for the door. She was one of the first people in the hallway and she hustled to her locker, anxious to leave. She spun the dial, landing on the familiar combination, and shoved her books into her backpack. Quickly, she slung her backpack over her shoulders, closing her locker.

On her way out of the school, she saw the flyer advertising the volleyball tryouts.

No way, she thought. She couldn't handle more embarrassment on top of today.

Chapter 28

FOOTSTEPS APPROACHED REAGAN'S BED. Wasn't anyone in her family capable of walking quietly? She gritted her teeth through her annoyance.

Her mom sat on the side of her bed, the weight of her body shifting Reagan's position. Her mom was watching her sleep, and Reagan wondered if her face was giving away her lie. A hand patted her hip lightly. "Reagan, sweetie," her mom whispered.

Reagan ignored her. Maybe if she feigned sleep long enough, her mom would leave her alone.

"Honey, it's time to get up," the hand on her hip patted softly. "You need to eat some food, and I need your help with something."

Reagan remained silent, deep inhales and exhales to mimic the rhythmic breathing of sleep.

"Reagan," her mom said again, this time louder. "I need you to come run an errand with me."

She pulled the covers off Reagan's body.

"Mom!" Reagan groaned.

"I know," her mom said. "I know you don't want to, but I need your help."

"With what?" Reagan asked warily.

"I need to get Cora some shorts and I don't know what's cool and what's not." Julie turned to the windows. "Let's get some light in here, shall we?" She opened the curtains and pulled the string for the blinds. Reagan watched as light poured in, coating everything in sight with a hopeful, bright hue.

If only it were that easy, Reagan thought. *If only I could pull the curtains and light would flood back into me.* She dug the palms of her hands into her eyes. Her mom sat on the bed next to her.

"Reagan," she said, lightly touching Reagan's elbow. "What's going on, honey? Your dad and I are worried about you." Her voice was gentle, filled with kindness.

Tears seeped from her eyes and through the cracks in her hands.

"I don't know what's going on," she admitted. "I just don't even care anymore. Getting out of bed takes too much energy. I hate everyone around me. I don't want to play soccer anymore. I don't want to do anything."

Julie wrapped her arms around her daughter, enveloping her body. For some reason, this made her cry harder, made her pain that much more acute. Reagan's heart swelled in response to the gentle gesture.

"This pain is a lot to carry, especially alone," her mom said through her tears.

"How do you do it?" Reagan asked. "How do you get up every day, and look at his room, and his things and live your life? Don't you just want to curl up in bed and never leave?"

"Most days, yes," Julie admitted. "Most days I wake up certain it was a terrible dream. And then reality sets in and I remember the nightmare we're living in right now."

"When will it get better?" Reagan asked, her face buried in the crook of her mom's elbow. Reagan's emotions were raw, exposed. Vulnerability was a side of her she tried to hide at all costs.

"I don't know," Julie replied. "I don't know that it will. I think we carry this with us like a bag of rocks for the rest of our lives."

The admission was strangely refreshing to Reagan; it was an acknowledgement that Reagan's life was forever altered, that the ripples would last forever.

Her mom pulled away, her hands on Reagan's shoulders.

"But Reags," she said, looking at Reagan in the eyes. Her eyes were wet and sad, but there was a familiar kindness there, too. "I know it's hard, but you've got to talk to us. And if you don't want to talk to us, we'll get someone that you do want to talk to. There is no shame in having sad feelings, no shame in having even darker feelings than that." Her mom paused, looking at her carefully. Reagan averted her eyes, ashamed to admit that she'd had suicidal thoughts. She gave a small nod.

"Do you know what happens when you carry a bag of rocks?" Her mom ducked her head so her eyes met Reagan's. Reagan shook her head.

"We get stronger. We develop different muscles and maybe the load gets easier to bear, one day, one step at a time." She paused, her eyes kind and gentle. "At least that's my hope."

Reagan nodded, and for the first time in many months, a ray of light pierced the darkest part of her soul and sparked the faintest glimmer of hope.

Her mom patted her knee and stood.

"Hop in the shower. We'll get a smoothie and run to the sporting goods store. Cora's going to try out for the volleyball team, and I don't think she even owns a pair of athletic shorts."

Reagan couldn't believe her ears. She stifled a laugh. "Cora?" She asked incredulously.

"She's excited," Julie said, a warning in her voice.

Reagan nodded and raised her arms above her head in a stretch. She couldn't remember the last time she ate, and her stomach grumbled.

"I'll see you downstairs," her mom said, kissing her forehead.

Reagan came down the stairs wearing jeans and a loose hoodie from her sophomore year of soccer. The sweatshirt was old and faded, but it was one of Reagan's favorites. Her last name and soccer number were emblazoned on the back.

Julie smiled when she walked into the kitchen. "You ready?" she asked.

"Yeah," Reagan said. She couldn't believe they were going to buy athletic shorts for the least athletic person in the entire world, but she kept that to herself.

"What do you think of these?" Julie held up a pair of hot pink running shorts with orange trim.

"I don't know, they're fine," Reagan said.

"Or would she like these better?" Julie said, as much to herself as Reagan. She held the shorts out in front of her, raising one arm while lowering the other, and then repeating the process on the other side.

"Those look more like her," Reagan said, motioning to the mint green pair in Julie's hand.

"Maybe I'll get her a few pairs," her mom said, absently. "If she makes the team, they'll practice, and she'll need more than one." She looked hopeful.

Reagan guffawed. "She's not going to make the team, Mom. No way." Reagan shook her head.

"Listen, I know she's not the most athletic girl, but no one is when they're that age. Plus, she's excited and she's interested. Maybe she will, I don't know," Julie said with a shrug.

"Whatever you want to do," she said.

Julie turned her attention back to the round rack in front of her, rifling through swishy shorts and trying to find Cora's size.

"Reagan?" There was a quiet voice behind her. Reagan turned to see Ellie, a teammate from her soccer team.

"Oh, hey, Ellie," Reagan said coolly, slurping her smoothie to avoid further conversation. She turned, but Ellie kept talking.

"Are you getting some new running shorts?" she asked, gesturing to the shorts in Julie's hand.

"No," Reagan replied. "Those are for my sister."

"Oh nice." Ellie opened her mouth as though to say something, but closed it again.

"See ya, Ellie," Reagan said. She turned her back, hoping Ellie would take the hint that she didn't want to talk.

"I just wanted to say I'm sorry about Buckhead," Ellie blurted out. "I'm really sorry. On top of everything you're going through, that must have been really hard."

Red-hot panic rose into Reagan's cheeks, and she scrambled to think of something, anything, to say. But her mind was blank and her mouth was frozen.

"Well, um, I'll see you around," Ellie said, as if realizing her error. She turned, walking away quickly.

Reagan kept her shoulders squared away from her mom. She couldn't bear to face her right now.

"Reagan," Julie said, quietly. Reagan braced herself for a lecture. For some maternal wisdom about how she had squandered this opportunity and would now have to live with the consequences. But when her mom spoke again, her voice was so gentle, it nearly brought Reagan to tears. "Let's get out of here," she said softly, lightly guiding Reagan's elbow to the cashier and then to the car.

When she had buckled her seatbelt, Reagan let out a dramatic exhale.

"Okay, Mom, let's get it over with," she said. "Yell at me and let's move on." She waited. Nothing. She put her head back against the seat and closed her eyes, waiting.

Julie shook her head. "I don't have anything to yell at you about," she said, quietly. "Ellie's comment... I assume it means there's no more scholarship?"

"Something like that," Reagan muttered. "The coach called me a couple of times, and I never replied. Coach Stradler called me and told me I was at risk of losing it, but I just didn't care. I don't care," she corrected.

Julie nodded, her eyes still ahead following the road ahead.

"Playing a collegiate sport is no small feat," her mom said. "One that takes an extraordinary commitment."

"I know, Mom," Reagan said, annoyed. "I've been playing competitive soccer my whole life. I know what it takes to make it to the collegiate level."

"All I'm saying is it's okay if you don't want to play anymore," Julie said, glancing at Reagan. "You've been through a lot, and it's normal if your interest in things changes as a result of that."

Reagan was silent.

"We can always figure out college, even without a scholarship," Julie continued. Guilt crept into Reagan's stomach. She hadn't even considered the financial burden a college education would be on her parents. She hadn't even considered that maybe they, too, were grateful for the scholarship for an entirely different reason.

"I don't want to go to college," Reagan said, enunciating each word so each sounded like an individual statement. "I just want to go home."

Reagan sat back in the seat, defeated. The tiny ray of hope from earlier was extinguished.

Chapter 29

CORA WAS NEVER MORE thankful for her mom's punctuality than she was today. Her mom was parked, waiting as soon as Cora stepped outside.

"Hey, hon." A plastic bag sat in her mom's lap, and she extended it to Cora when Cora sat down. "Look what I bought today." Julie beamed.

Cora opened the bag, saw the running shorts inside, and closed it quickly.

"I'm not trying out for the team," she said quietly.

"Oh," Julie stammered. "Why not?"

"I just changed my mind," Cora said, unable to raise her eyes from the plastic bag now sitting in her lap.

They rode the rest of the car ride home in silence. Cora ruminated the day's events over and over again in her mind. Her mom looked lost in thought, too.

When they got home, Cora quickly unbuckled her seatbelt, hurrying inside.

"Want a snack?" her mom called.

Cora shook her head, walking straight for the office. She turned around quickly.

"Can I Google something really quick?" she asked.

"Of course, honey," her mom answered, her eyes concerned. "Need help with anything?"

"No, just something I want to try drawing."

At the office computer, her fingers found the keys and she typed *Wahiba Sands*. Instantly, pictures populated her computer screen. The copper desert stretched against the backdrop of a crisp, blue sky. Sand dunes stood tall, grain by grain swept by the wind into waist-high pillars. The waves in the sand looked like they had been made by a machine, precise and uniform.

She saw camel caravans and rustic looking tents. She selected a picture of the vast desert and hit print. The printer rumbled awake, and then slowly printed the image. Once it was spit out by the printer, Cora snatched it from the tray and hurried up the stairs.

When they got home from the sporting goods store, Reagan stalked straight from the car to her bed. She kicked off her shoes and climbed under the covers, still wearing her jeans. Hot tears seeped from her eyes. She wasn't sure what had triggered this release of emotion, but the tears came like a tidal wave from deep inside her and there was no way of stopping them.

Ellie couldn't have known that no one in her family knew about Buckhead, but Reagan was furious that she'd brought it up. She was disappointed in herself, too. She wished her mom had yelled and screamed, but she hadn't. She had been kind and understanding, which made Reagan feel worse.

Her phone buzzed from her back pocket. Reagan retrieved it and saw a familiar name on her screen—Coach Stradler. He was the only person who called her anymore. She swiped to decline the call. She couldn't talk to him right now. She wiped the tears from her face with the backs of her hands. She had to go to the bathroom and then she was ready for a long nap.

She opened her bedroom door as Cora came up the stairs.

Cora looked embarrassed. "Hi," she said quietly, taking a big step to the far side of the hallway to avoid Reagan.

"Hi," Reagan said, coolly, and watched her younger sister walk down the hall. "Mom said you're trying out for the volleyball team," she said to her sister's back. Cora stopped walking and turned around to meet Reagan's gaze. The corners of Reagan's mouth curled up into a cruel sneer.

"Good luck," she scoffed. "If those coaches have ever seen you walk, they'll save themselves the time and cut you immediately."

She gave Cora a sickly-sweet smile and walked into the bathroom, closing the door behind her.

Chapter 30

CORA'S FACE BLAZED HOT. Reagan's words stung more than anything else that day, and now, despite the new pairs of athletic shorts waiting downstairs, despite the encouragement from Max, despite her mom's enthusiasm, Cora knew she could never step foot on a volleyball court.

Tears pricked her eyes, pooling and spilling onto her cheeks. Cora threw her backpack to the floor and it landed with a thud. She sat on her bed and curled her legs into her chest, wrapping her arms around her knees until she was a tight ball. She made herself as small as possible, imagining herself sinking into the soft down of her blankets. She wondered if Reagan's words stung more because they were mean, or if it was because they were true. She didn't know. But she did know there was no way she was going to try out for the volleyball team.

Eventually, Cora uncurled herself and picked her backpack off the floor. The picture of Wahiba Sands was smashed underneath the weight of her books, and the paper lay crumpled on her bedroom floor.

Cora picked it up, smoothing the paper against her desk, trying to iron out the folds. She unloaded her books into a neat pile and checked her agenda for her homework. Most of her teachers had given her leniency when it came to assignments, but Cora didn't need it. She liked having a reason to stay busy, keep her mind off Max. She made a quick list of her homework, placing small boxes next to each task that she could fill with a check mark once the assignment was complete.

A knock at the door startled her. "Cora?" Her mom's voice was muffled behind the closed door.

She opened the door to find her mom standing there with the plastic bag from the sporting goods store in her hands.

"Here are the shorts," she said, handing the bag to Cora. "I know you don't want to try out anymore, but it's good to have these anyway."

Cora took the bag and dropped it on her bed.

"Dinner will be ready in a few minutes," Julie said. "Come down in five?"

Cora nodded and went back to her desk, absorbing the details of the desert scene in front of her. When she went downstairs to the kitchen, her parents were speaking in hushed tones.

"I don't know details. I just know that there is no scholarship and she said she doesn't want to play anymore," her mom said quietly.

"Jules, we need to do something," her dad said. "This is not like her."

"I know, Ned. I know." Her mom's voice was exasperated. "I just don't know what to do."

Max's words echoed in Cora's mind. *She's struggling more than anyone realizes.*

Cora turned and hurried to her room. She grabbed the yellow bracelet from her desk, then braced herself and knocked gently on Reagan's door.

Chapter 31

LIVING IN SILENCE FOR the past few months had heightened Reagan's sense of hearing. She was attuned to listening, determining if someone was stopping at her door or carrying on. From the heavy thud of footsteps on the stairs, Reagan knew Cora was coming. Cora walked right past her door.

Good, Reagan thought. *The last person I want to deal with is Cora.*

A few minutes later, Reagan heard something rustling under her door and a soft knock. Reagan's phone buzzed. A white banner with the name Ellie Johnson and a soccer ball popped up on her phone, indicating a new text message.

Reagan slid her thumb over the screen, and the entire message popped up.

"Hey, I hope I didn't make anything awkward between you and your mom about the Buckhead thing. I didn't think about that until now. Anyway, hope you're okay. We miss you." She'd added a string of red and black hearts, their school colors.

Now that she'd had time to think about it, Reagan didn't really care about Ellie, or that she had inadvertently spilled the college beans to Reagan's mom. Or lack of college beans. Her announcement to Reagan and her mom had actually spared Reagan a difficult conversation.

But reality was starting to set in. If Reagan didn't go to college, what next? Was she bound to stay in this tiny shoebox room for the rest of her life? The thought made her feel claustrophobic, like she needed to get out. *Maybe a shower will help,* she thought.

On her way to the bathroom, her foot landed on something hard. She carried it to the bathroom, flipped on the bathroom light, and peered at the small mound in her hand. She held it up by one side and watched a bracelet take shape. She looked at the beads, looked at each letter of her name. The bracelet was obviously homemade with little ends of the clear string poking out at the ends, but Reagan also noted the careful placement and symmetry of the colors and letters. It was a cheap bracelet, but the small gesture made Reagan inexplicably sad and tender towards Cora.

She closed her mouth, stifling a cry, though tears still managed to spring from her eyes. She turned the shower on hot and stood under the shower head. The water hit her shoulders and back, and Reagan couldn't help but think that the weight of the water pounding against her skin actually felt lighter than the weight she normally bore.

Chapter 32

CORA SET HER SKETCHBOOK on the table and turned a few pages. She leafed past the lush jungle, past the narrow slot canyons, past the arch. Memories flooded her with the turn of each page. She stopped at the page of the windswept sand dunes and pushed the sketchpad across the table.

Her mom and dad sat on the other side of the table, and they reached for the sketchpad simultaneously, pulling it toward them.

"Wow," her dad said quietly, taking in every inch of the page. "Cora, this is really something special."

Cora shrugged. The truth was, it wasn't the drawing that was enticing to her, it was Max.

As her parents flipped through the pages of her sketchpad, Cora knew the gnawing in her stomach was guilt. She knew her parents would give anything to spend more time with Max, and somehow, she was able to. She swallowed hard, burying the guilt rising in her chest.

"How do you find these places?" her dad asked.

She shrugged again. "The forest was just something I came up with, and the slot canyon was a family vacation Mia went on. We had to research New Zealand for a class project, and I saw a picture of Wahiba Sands at school and just wondered if I could recreate it."

She sat back in her chair.

"I love that you have this creative outlet," her dad said, tapping the sketchpad with his index finger.

Cora shrugged again, deflecting the attention. Her face tingled and blushed with the focused attention on her.

"So where is this place? Where is Wahiba Sands?" He pulled his phone out of his back pocket.

He looked to Cora for an answer before typing with his thumbs.

"I don't know," she said. "I just liked the way it looked."

"Oman," he answered. He turned his phone toward her, showing her the small square screen.

It looked less impressive on a small phone screen, but still magnificent to Cora. Her dad turned his phone again, showing Cora's mom.

"Wow," she breathed quietly. "That's beautiful. And I can really see the resemblance in your drawing." She flashed Cora a smile, and Cora smiled back.

"I should know this," her dad said, sheepishly. "But are you in an art class?"

Cora shook her head. "Not right now. Next semester, once electives change." She already knew the art studio would be a sanctuary, one of the few places she was comfortable.

Her dad nodded. "Yeah, changing electives," he said slowly, as if remembering his own middle-school days. "I was the opposite. I always dreaded the change into an art class." He winked at her.

"What elective did you like, then?" Cora asked. It was weird thinking her parents were ever her age.

Her dad leaned back in his chair, thoughtfully. "What elective did I like? I always liked my math classes, hence why I became an accountant." He opened his hands as if it was an obvious connection, math and accounting.

Cora winced at the mention of math class, and Ned noticed.

"I take it from your reaction that you don't enjoy math," he said.

"I'm not very good at math," she said, her head down, examining her fingernails.

"Math can be tricky."

Not only did she hate math, but now she didn't even like thinking about it, remembering all the embarrassment caused by that dumb protractor.

"What are you learning about right now?" he asked, ignoring her silence.

"Angles?" Cora guessed. "Something to do with protractors. I was following along, and then Mrs. Courtney just went too fast, and I got lost and confused."

Her dad nodded, sympathetic. "I hated geometry, too. Want to show me what you're working on now?"

Cora hesitated. She did have homework, and it would be nice to have her dad's help. But she was also desperate to get upstairs and work on her sketchpad. But the idea of another humiliating protractor experience with anyone from her math class was enough motivation to accept her dad's help.

"That would be awesome. Thanks Dad," Cora said. "My stuff is upstairs. I'll run and grab it."

She raced to the top of the stairs, careful to slow her pace when she passed Reagan's room. She wondered if Reagan had found the bracelet yet. Her room was dark and quiet, and Cora wondered if she was already asleep.

She grabbed her textbook and math notebook from her desk and walked down the hall, pausing in front of Reagan's room. Despite all of Reagan's cruel jabs and insults, Cora felt sorry for her. Reagan looked miserable all the time, and basically lived in her room. Before Max died, Reagan had gone to school every day purely for the social aspects. To walk in the crowded hallways, to see her friends. Now that motivation was gone, and so was the motivation to go to school. Cora could see glimpses of what Max had told her, that Reagan was struggling more than any of them knew.

After an hour of concentrated math help, Cora was starting to have a grasp on the concept. Her dad was patient, taking time to explain along the way, and giving her ample opportunity to try solving the problems on her own, intervening when she made a mistake. They finished the assignment, and Cora sat back, triumphant.

"Awesome job, sweetie," her dad said, kissing the top of her head. "That took a lot of patience." He raised his hands over his head in an over-the-top cheering gesture.

Cora laughed. "Thanks, Dad. It makes a lot more sense now."

Ned closed her book and nodded. "I'm glad. Math really isn't that bad. But it can get confusing at times. Plus, it's all up here." He tapped the side of his head with his finger.

"What's up there?" Cora asked, confused.

"You believe what you tell yourself," he said, looking at her. "If you tell yourself you're bad at math enough times, you'll start to believe it. If you tell yourself you're a hard worker and you work to solve problems, you'll do that too."

Cora was quiet, and her dad continued.

"Your brain is a very powerful tool, honey," he said, stacking her math papers on her book. "A lot of people don't realize that."

Her mom appeared with two small bowls of ice cream.

"Okay math wizards, ready for some ice cream?" She set the bowls down in front of them, placing spoons in the bowls with a soft clink.

They ate in silence, the light clatter of their spoons the only sound. Cora thought of Reagan upstairs.

"Should I go get Reagan? Maybe she would like some ice cream, too." Cora asked.

A look of shock flashed across her mom's face before it was quickly replaced by a smile.

"That's very sweet of you, Cora," she said, reaching across the table and patting Cora's hand. "I think that's a great idea."

Cora walked up the stairs quietly, suddenly second guessing her decision. She reached the top of the stairs and after a few more steps, stood in front of Reagan's door. She leaned toward the door listening for sounds of life. Nothing. She knocked lightly. Nothing. Cora took a deep breath, slowly opening the door. Reagan's room was pitch black. She took a few steps towards the bed. Reagan's chest rose and fell in rhythmic motion, her breathing steady.

"Reagan?" She whispered, inching closer. Her face was turned toward Cora, her head resting on her arm. Cora was filled with compassion for her older sister, when she wasn't spewing insults and jabs. Cora turned to leave, making a personal resolve to find a way to connect with Reagan.

Chapter 33

CORA INHALED AND IMMEDIATELY regretted it. Hot, dry air filled her lungs. She stretched her fingers out and touched the ground beneath her. She didn't remember falling asleep, but here she was, in the middle of the desert. Fine sand, baked by the sun singed her fingertips.

She sat up slowly, taking in the vast skyline ahead of her. Windswept sand dunes dotted the horizon as far as Cora could see. The heat was unbearable, with no shade in sight. A trail of sweat trickled down the back of her neck.

Cora waited for Max, sweltering in the sun. The wind had blown patterns in the sand, intricate designs that looked like a meticulous machine had made them. Cora raised her arm to shield her face from the sun. She stood, looking for any sign of Max. As she rose, she saw a message. "Find me in the dunes," was scrawled in the sand.

"What?" Cora said aloud, incredulous. "Which one?"

Her gaze flicked across the horizon, searching for Max. A building stood in the distance. The top right window of the building was illuminated by a green-gold glow.

How had she missed that before? It stood tall and wide, out of place in the middle of the desert. She walked toward the building, anxious to find Max. Her tongue felt like carpet inside her mouth. She was desperate for a sip of water.

The building appeared to float just above the horizon. Cora shook her head. *Buildings don't float.* She was dehydrated, fatigued, and now she was hallucinating. The problem was, she was alone, stuck in the middle of a sandy desert, unable to discern what was real and what was a mirage. She rubbed her eyes and opened them again. The building was gone, but just beyond her gaze was a pool of crystal blue water. She pushed onward. She knew water in the middle of the desert was probably unsafe to drink, but maybe she could at least cool her skin.

When she got closer, the pool of water vanished before her eyes. She circled, feeling alone and exposed, then crumpled into a defeated heap in the middle of the desert, unsure of where to go, or what to do next.

Cora let herself wallow there, gathering her strength and trying to formulate a plan. With no water and no shade in sight, her time in the desert was extremely limited. She clenched the compass in her hand and squeezed her eyes shut, but to no avail. She wasn't surprised. The compass always took her back when she least expected it. She was reminded of the sandy message. *Find me in the dunes*. It was time to find Max.

In front of her, another image took shape. This time, the image was familiar, unmistakable. It was her home, the familiar green light emanating from Max's bedroom window. Cora hesitated, unable to discern her next movement. Max said to find him in the dunes, but the green light beckoned her. It had led her to the compass, after all. She deliberated, paralyzed, unable to decide. She rubbed her eyes, jarring the mirage, and stepped toward the dunes.

Cora wasn't sure how much time had actually passed, but time seemed to drag on in the desert as she peered behind sand dunes in search of Max. Her body ached, each step heavier than the last. She sank against a sand dune, her head in her hands.

"Cora! You made it!" Max's voice came from behind her. "I was starting to think you might have gotten lost."

"Where were you? Why didn't you help me?" Cora said angrily.

"I had to stand back and let you see that you are so much more capable than you think." He sat beside her in the sand.

"You made me do that all by myself. I thought I was going to die."

"That's what being brave is, Cora. It's being scared and doing something anyway. That's what you've been doing all along. That's what we've been practicing."

"Practicing for what?" Cora asked.

"I need you to realize the power you have within you. You had everything you needed already inside. You just needed someone to show you."

"Why did you trick me?" Cora yelled, exasperated. "I thought I saw the building, but it turned out to be a mirage. I was so confused." Cora let out a defeated whimper.

"What building?" Max asked. He looked around, confused.

"The building with the green window? It was the same building where I found your compass. I thought you led me to it." Cora's voiced trailed off when she saw the confusion on Max's face. He shook his head.

"A building? I don't know anything about a building. I did leave my compass for you, but I left it in your sweatshirt pocket. I wanted you to have it, and I didn't want someone else to find it. I thought leaving it in your sweatshirt was the safest way to get it to you."

Disappointment and confusion washed over Cora, drowning her like a tidal wave. This whole time she thought Max had led her to the compass, had been trying to communicate with her. She was devastated at the thought that this was all just a coincidence. She swallowed hard, trying to suppress her tears.

"Have you ever wondered why you, and only you, have the ability to see me?" Max asked her.

She shrugged, toying with the compass tucked safely underneath her shirt.

"It's only partly to do with that." Max answered her silent question and Cora's face burned with embarrassment that he knew she had the compass all along. "You're creating something new, Cora. You're creating a transformed version of yourself. This experience, this grief, is changing you into something different, something better."

Cora's thoughts were jumbled, turned upside down as she struggled to piece together what Max was telling her.

"Do you know what alchemy is?" Max asked. Cora shook her head.

"It's an ancient practice, almost like chemistry." His eyes were trained on the horizon, where the desert sand met the darkening night sky. "Alchemists tried to change base metals into gold, that they could then turn into a magic elixir."

"A magic elixir," Cora repeated skeptically.

"The magic is in the transformation, not the elixir. They turned metal into something even more valuable. You're being transformed in these worlds, Cora. These experiences are preparing you for something epic."

"Epic is a loaded word, Max," Cora said.

"It's just a collection of tiny decisions that build and build upon each other that create an epic life. You aren't born a brave person, but you become brave by doing little brave things every single day. By asking someone new to sit with you at lunch. By trying out for the volleyball team, maybe."

"But how?" Cora uttered. "How is this possible?" She motioned to their surroundings.

"You," Max answered. "You're the real power. It's already within you. You just had to see it for yourself. The compass is just a way of transportation. But you, you're the real power."

"How does it work?" Cora slipped the compass over her neck, examining the gold ball in the palm of her hand. The gold was lustrous tonight, practically beaming in her hand. She flipped the compass over as if searching for the answer there.

"Think about all the experiences we've had," Max said, prodding her to discover the answer on her own.

"I found the compass at the top of the waterfall and ended up back home, in bed." She held up the string holding the compass, as if the answer were right in front of her.

"But what happened right before you found the compass? Do you remember?"

"Yes, how could I forget? We climbed up the side of the mountain," she said, flatly.

"You climbed up the side of the mountain, yes," Max agreed, nodding. "Okay, what about the next adventure?" His eyes were fixed on her.

"I don't know, Max," she said, looking away.

"Yes, you do," he nudged. "What happened in the slot canyon?"

"I caught the compass! It was going to fall out of my shorts pocket, and I caught it. And then magically, I was back in bed!"

"But what happened right before that?"

Cora shook her head, exasperated. "I don't know, Max! I don't know what you're trying to make me understand!"

She was frustrated, but Max wasn't letting it go.

"I need you to understand what the power actually is that gets you back home, gets you to safety," he said softly, but with a fierce intensity. "It's not the compass. The compass is a tool to transport you, yes. But there is something that happens right before, every single time, and that's not the power of the compass. That's the power of you." He pointed to her.

"Max," she said, dropping her head again. "I know you think I'm capable of all these amazing things, but I'm really not."

"Cora," Max said. He was silent until her eyes met his. "You are the force. The pinnacle of power within you is the moment you overcome your fear. Looking back, can you see that? Can you see that within yourself?"

He was partly right; she was scared of heights and scaled the side of a mountain, she was scared of being swept away by the current and found a solution, she was scared of dark, open water and she managed to face that fear.

"Don't you see, Cora? Don't you see where the real power is?" Max's voice was quiet, a near whisper. "It's you. Everything you need is already apart of you."

Darkness settled around them, still seated on the hot desert sand. The constellations hung in the sky above them. Max settled back, his arms draped casually over his knees.

"Only in darkness can we see the stars. Darkness gives us a reason to look for hope." Max tilted his head, looking into the heavens above. "I like the way that sounds, but the darkness can be scary. Sometimes it's hard to notice the stars," Cora said quietly. She looked around, gazing out at the inky night sky around her. "If the only way I get back home is by overcoming something, then what obstacle do I have to overcome here?" She looked around. The sky was black, and the desert was empty. There was no threat in sight.

Max was quiet beside her. His gaze was fixed on something far in the distance, and when he turned to look at Cora, his eyes were filled with tears. She knew then, in that moment, that the one thing she feared the very most, was losing someone again. She forced herself to look at Max even though it hurt. She wanted to memorize every detail, every line on his face. She wanted the sound of his laugh imprinted on her memory forever.

"You've learned everything you can from me," Max said. A bright smile remained on his face, despite tears filling his eyes. "Someone very close to you, to us, needs a lot of help. And I can't help her, but you can."

Reagan. In the days leading up to today, there'd been a constant nagging in Cora's head that she couldn't quite place. But now, here with Max, she understood exactly what it was. It was Reagan.

"How do I help her?" Cora asked quietly.

"I don't know the answer to that, but you do," Max said. "Or you will. I do know that if you take a step forward, if you take a step of faith into the unknown, you will always be rewarded. Like with bioluminescent glowworms."

"I'm not ready," she stammered. "I don't want to leave."

"You're never going to feel ready," Max reminded her. "That's where your bravery comes in. That's where you have to find that one second of courage and seize it with everything you have. You grab hold of it and you don't let go, because when you lose your courage is when you begin to sink. This is it, Cora. This is the moment."

Cora looked at him expectantly, her eyes pleading for one more minute.

"I can't wait to watch your epic life." His eyes twinkled.

Cora found it then, the flickering flame of courage. Before it could flitter away, she seized it. She clasped her hand around the compass and squeezed her eyes shut, forcing hot tears onto her cheeks.

Chapter 34

REAGAN WAS FAMILIAR WITH the creaks and groans as the house settled into slumber. But this night, something was different. The house wasn't as still as it normally was.

She opened her bedroom door. A small sliver of light from behind Max's door spilled into the hallway. Reagan tiptoed down the hall, wondering who she would find behind Max's closed door. Tentatively, she opened the door. Julie's head snapped toward her as the door opened. Julie's eyes were red, tears still damp on her face. She didn't say anything, just looked at Reagan with sad eyes.

"I had to go to the bathroom and saw Max's light was on. I didn't know you'd be in here." Reagan hesitated in the doorway.

Julie motioned her in, still lying on the bed.

"Normally I try to stay away from this room," she said as Reagan made her way across the room. "But tonight... I don't know. I guess I just wanted to feel close to him."

Reagan understood. "I was in here, too, the other night. I guess I was looking for the same thing." Reagan sat on the edge of the bed, her arms wrapped tightly around her chest. Julie pulled Reagan's elbow, drawing her further onto the bed. Reagan succumbed quickly, nestling her body into the crook of Julie's.

Reagan listened to their breathing, waiting for her mom to say something. When she didn't, Reagan broke the silence.

"Mom?" Reagan whispered, her face turned away from Julie's. "I'm sorry about Buckhead."

Julie stroked Reagan's hair. "Don't be sorry," she said, finally. "We're not mad. We'll figure something out." Her hand moved steadily over Reagan's hair. Reagan's body relaxed.

"What happens next?" Reagan asked. "What do I do next?"

"You don't have to know what comes next," Julie answered. "You don't have to have everything figured out right this second."

"But what about college? What if I can't get a scholarship anywhere else? What if I don't want to play soccer anywhere? My grades definitely aren't good enough to get a scholarship to any school." Reagan's thoughts reeled with uncertainty.

"What about college?" Julie asked her. "Is that something you want to do right now? Do you want to take some time off?"

"I don't know," Reagan said softly. "Some days I do. Some days I just want to get out of this place. Get out of all the reminders of Max. Get away from all of the sadness and just start over where no one knows my story."

"I understand that," Julie murmured. "Sometimes I wish I could start over, too."

"But some days I don't even want to get out of bed, or shower, or leave my room." Reagan's voice cracked.

"I understand that, too," Julie said.

"I feel really guilty. I feel guilty that I get to experience all these big things, like graduating and going to college and all those things, and Max never will."

"Reagan," Julie said softly. "The last thing Max would want you to do is to wallow in sadness. He would want you out there, living a life big enough for the both of you. I know that with everything in me."

Reagan's breath caught in her throat. "I don't know how to feel like myself again," she said quietly.

"I don't know that you ever will feel like your old self," Julie admitted, both to herself and to Reagan. "I think that's part of what makes grief so hard. You can't ever go back to the way things were. Grief changes you."

Reagan was quiet on the bed next to her.

"And what if I don't want to play soccer again? Then what do I do?" Reagan whispered, barely able to audibly utter the words.

Julie smiled at the ceiling. "Believe it or not, there are other things to life than soccer."

"But soccer is my thing. Without soccer, I'm nothing." Reagan said.

"You're good at soccer, yes. You have worked very hard at soccer, yes. But what your *thing* is, what sets you apart? That's not soccer. That comes from deep inside you. That comes from the very soul of you."

"How do I know what that is, though?" Reagan asked.

"It takes time to figure that out," Julie said. "It takes experience and looking inward. Asking yourself what makes you feel the very most like the person you were meant to be. It's not always something you just know, right off the bat."

Reagan asked very quietly, "What makes you feel most like yourself?"

The question caught Julie off guard, and she hesitated but answered truthfully.

"I don't know anymore, sweetie," she said, still stroking Reagan's hair. Long, blond strands were splayed out on the bed. "I may need to do some searching, too."

Chapter 35

CORA WOKE, DETERMINED. SHE scrambled out of bed and hurried to shower. She dressed and brushed her teeth, then filled her backpack with the books she needed for that day. On her way out the door, she grabbed the plastic bag of athletic shorts. She bounded down the stairs.

"Morning, Mom," she said brightly. "I changed my mind. I'm going to try out for the volleyball team today," she said resolutely.

Her mom blinked, surprised.

"I-I-I-" she stammered, clearly caught off guard. "I think that's a great idea." She gave Cora a wide, enthusiastic smile.

"You know," Julie said, a rubber spatula in one hand, her eyes locked on the bubbling pancakes on the griddle. "I was a cheerleader when I was younger, but I always wanted to play the sports, not cheer on the sidelines."

"Why didn't you play them, then?" Cora asked. It was strange to think of her mom as anyone except her mom. Even more strange to think of her mom as someone like herself, her own age.

Her mom shrugged and flipped over a pancake. "I never really had the opportunity, I guess," she said. "Or maybe I just was too nervous. I was a very anxious little kid."

"Really?" Cora was surprised. "How did you get over it?"

Her mom shrugged and furrowed her eyebrows together, thinking. "Good question," she said. "I don't know that I got over it as much as I just realized it didn't matter as much as I thought it did. The older you get, the more comfortable you become with who you are."

"But when was that?" Cora pressed.

"Oh, boy," Julie said, blowing the air out of her mouth. "I don't really remember. I think it was a gradual process, you know? Just getting older and wiser, I guess."

"So, did you ever try playing a sport?" Cora asked.

"Nope, I never did," her mom said, flipping the two pancakes onto a plate. "I never had enough courage to put myself out there like that, to try something new."

Cora nodded, digesting the information her mom was sharing with her. Discovering this tidbit was like unearthing a small fleck of gold, a common thread that bound them together.

"It's one of the reasons I think you trying out for the volleyball team is so great." She handed Cora the plate stacked with pancakes. "Imagine what's possible, what's out there, when you let go of doubt? I wish I had tried more things when I was younger. It's a lesson I'm still learning."

She turned, placing the batter bowl in the sink and turning the water on hot. Cora stabbed at her pancakes and shoveled them into her mouth. She was anxious to get the day going. Her mom turned to her from the sink.

"So, tryouts are at three?"

Cora nodded, chewing a mouthful of pancakes.

"Any idea what time they're done?" Julie asked.

Cora shook her head.

"Okay." Her mom turned the water off in the sink. "I can call the school and ask."

Cora swallowed. "What do you think the tryouts will be like?" she asked quietly.

Her mom cocked her head slightly, then crossed the kitchen. She slid into the tall chair next to Cora and put her arm around the back of Cora's chair.

"From what I've learned with Reagan and Max, every tryout is a little different, but at this level, they all have one thing in common," she explained. "The coaches just want to see that you can work hard, that you're teachable, and that you don't give up."

Cora looked down at her hands in her lap and nodded.

"So, I assume they'll have you guys warm up, maybe run some laps around the gym, then maybe do some volleyball drills," her mom said.

"I'm nervous," she said quietly, picking at the skin near her fingernails.

"Cora." Her mom lifted her chin so their eyes met. "It's totally normal to be nervous. Reagan still gets nervous before a tryout, and I'll tell you the same thing I tell her when she's nervous. Sometimes you'll make the team, sometimes you won't. You can only control how you show up. Try your best, stay positive, leave it all on the court." She smiled at Cora, and Cora gave her a weak smile in return.

"I'm proud of you," she said, pulling Cora's head in and kissing her forehead. "You're going to do great."

Cora noticed tears pooling in her mom's eyes, but she brushed them away quickly.

"Max would be proud of you, too," she said. "He was always your biggest fan."

The mention of Max's name from her mother's mouth made Cora's heart leap. Her mom didn't say his name often, and when she did, it was cracked and filled with emotion. This time, however, her voice was strong, solid.

"Thanks for breakfast, Mom. I'll be right down." She needed a way to channel Max's confidence for tryouts.

She ran up the stairs, tiptoeing past Reagan's room, and found a sticky note pad on her desk.

You've already not made the team. She scribbled the phrase on a note, folded it into tiny quarters, and slipped it into her pocket. There. She would carry Max's wisdom with her throughout the day.

She bound down the stairs and grabbed her backpack and the plastic bag filled with her tryout clothes.

"Okay, I'm ready," she said. When she came back down, Ned stood smiling in the kitchen.

"Good morning, and good luck," he said, cheerily. "I think it's really cool you're trying out for the team. I can't wait to hear about it." He kissed the top of her head.

"Ready?" her mom asked. She stood near the garage door, keys in hand.

You've already not made the team, Cora reminded herself as she climbed in the car and rode to school.

Chapter 36

REAGAN STRETCHED IN HER bed, reaching her arms up and over her head, holding her muscles taut for a second before releasing. A sigh escaped her lips as she relaxed her muscles. She thought about the night before, cuddled with her mom in one, singular lump on Max's old bed. Her mom spoke of her pain, her loss, and her grief. Reagan had listened mutely, but her thoughts were on the compass. She'd wanted to scour Max's room again, but she'd refrained. When the house was quiet again—when Cora was at school, her dad was at work, and her mom was running errands—Reagan would find that compass.

A ball of worried nerves had sat in Cora's belly all day. She glanced at the clock on the wall. The minute hand inched forward. She tried to focus on the lessons, but her thoughts were consumed with the impending tryouts.

She dug for the folded paper in her pocket and pulled it out. It was crumpled and the corners had turned indigo from the dye of her jeans. She opened it discreetly, reading the words she had written to herself.

You've already not made the team.

She read the words over and over again. They offered a quiet reassurance when she doubted herself, which was nearly all day today.

The bell rang and Cora gathered her book and notebook into a neat stack, sliding it off her desk. She walked quickly to her locker, shoving her books in and pulling out her shorts. Mia appeared at her locker with a happy smile.

"Ready to go?" she asked.

Cora winced. She hadn't planned to tell Mia, or anyone, about the volleyball tryouts.

"I'm actually trying out for the volleyball team today," Cora said, a little sheepishly.

"What! How did I not know you played volleyball?" Mia asked.

"I don't. I mean, I haven't. But I saw the sign and kinda wanted to try." She shrugged and looked at her friend.

"Good luck!" A wide grim was plastered on her face. "You'll do awesome!"

Mia's confidence in her was encouraging, and Cora felt a surge of love for her best friend.

"Thanks." Cora grimaced a bit. "I'm starting to have second thoughts."

She watched as a throng of sporty-looking girls giggled their way to the bathroom, duffel bags slung over their shoulders. She swallowed.

Mia noticed Cora's eyes and followed her gaze.

"Hey, don't be nervous," she said, bringing her gaze back to Cora. "You're going to do great. And who knows, maybe you'll find something new you love!"

"Yeah, maybe." Cora nodded and glanced at the clock on the wall.

"I gotta go find my mom, but good luck," Mia said, folding Cora into a hug. Always unsure of what to do with her arms, Cora lightly patted Mia's back, instantly uncomfortable with her decision. "Let me know how it goes!" Mia said.

"I will for sure," Cora said, forcing a smile.

Mia waved and Cora watched her friend walk down the hallway, the crowd of students already dispersing.

Cora hesitated in the hallway, pretending to fiddle with her locker. She hoped the sporty girls would change quickly and she could have the bathroom alone, but they hadn't emerged, and Cora was anxious about the time. She would have to change with all of them in the bathroom. She pulled open the door and was met with a chorus of laughter and exclamations. Two of the girls were already changed and sat on the bathroom counter. Two were sequestered in stalls, exchanging their school clothes for gym shorts and T-shirts.

Cora fingered the hem of her cotton T-shirt, feeling insecure and out of place. She ducked into a stall quickly before they could notice her. Sitting on the toilet, she kicked off her shoes and pulled off her jeans. She slipped the shorts on and cringed at how high they came on her legs. She balled up her jeans and tried to sneak out of the bathroom, but she was spotted.

"Hey," a voice said as Cora crept out of the stall. "Are you trying out for the volleyball team?"

Cora turned, her cheeks automatically turning pink. The girl hoisted herself off the counter and reached Cora in a few steps. She had dark brown hair set in a high ponytail on the top of her head. She wore brand new running shoes.

Cora nodded and dropped her eyes to her own pink high-top sneakers. She was out of place in her street shoes and plain T-shirt.

"Cool," she said, facing Cora. "I'm Sophie. These girls are Danika, Chloe, and Addie." She said, gesturing to the girls behind her. They stood at the counter, tightening their ponytails.

"What's your name?" Sophie asked Cora. Her smile was warm and genuine, and Cora couldn't help but smile back.

"Cora," she answered quietly.

"Nice to meet you," Sophie answered brightly. She gestured to Cora's hair. "Do you need an extra hair tie? I have one." She pulled a stretchy band from her wrist and handed it to Cora.

Cora flushed. Her hair. Her wild, frizzy hair. She hadn't even thought about how she would contain it. She reached her hand forward, accepting the elastic band.

"Thanks," she said.

"No problem," she said, still smiling. She stood there for a second longer, maybe waiting for Cora to say something. But Cora was mute. She was taken aback by Sophie's outgoing nature, by her kindness and confidence. Sophie glanced at her watch.

"Actually, we should probably get out there," she said as much to Cora as to Danika, Chloe, and Addie. From their places in front of the mirror, they all murmured consent, giving their ponytails a final tug.

"I'm going to put my jeans in my locker," Cora managed. "I'll see you in there."

She hurried to her locker, jumbled the combination, and shoved her jeans in.

"Max," she whispered. "Help me."

She slammed her locker shut and walked quickly to the gym doors before she could change her mind.

Chapter 37

THE SMELL OF THE middle-school gym filled her nostrils, a combination of cleaning solution and rubber athletic equipment.

Across the gym, Cora's eyes found a group of girls huddled in the corner. At the opening of the door, the coach turned his head.

"Volleyball?" he yelled the question.

Cora nodded.

"Hustle over then!" His voice boomed. "You're late."

Cora's heart quickened and she glanced at the clock—3:01. She pulled her hair back as she walked, using the hair band Sophie had offered. The coach turned, and Cora realized he was waiting for her before continuing. She broke into a jog.

"What's your name?" he asked when Cora arrived.

"Cora," she replied, a bit breathless from both the jog and the anxiety of it all.

"Last name?" He wore athletic shoes and black pants that swished when he walked, as well as a worn sweatshirt with a school logo she didn't recognize.

"Jones."

He scribbled her name down on a clipboard.

"All right, Cora." He pointed to a spot at the end of the line. "Stand there. We're just going over what to expect today and tomorrow."

Cora made eye contact with Sophie who gave her another smile. She offered a sheepish smile in return.

"As I was saying," the coach continued. "I'm Coach Parrish. The next two days will be fairly run of the mill. Drills, skills tests, that sort of thing. You don't have to be the best volleyball player in the world to make the team, but we are looking for someone with these three things."

He held up three meaty fingers.

"One. We're looking for someone who works hard. Like I said, you don't have to be the best volleyball player in the world, but if you're willing to work hard, you can do great things. So that's number one." He dropped a finger, indicating there were two things left.

"Two. We're looking for someone who is willing to learn. I know I just said you don't have to be the best, but if you happen to be the best and you aren't willing to learn, we'll cut you from the team." He dropped another finger.

"And the last thing, and maybe the most important thing, that we're looking for is someone who doesn't give up. Someone who is willing to get back up if they fall down. Someone who is willing to put it all out there," He looked at a petite blonde that Cora had somehow missed, standing in the corner. "Tracey, am I missing anything?" he asked.

She shook her head, smiling and holding another clipboard against her chest. "I don't think so, no," she said, still smiling.

"Okay. This is my wife, and she's going to be helping me with tryouts," Coach Parrish explained, gesturing to the blonde. "You can just call her Mrs. Parrish."

"Call me Tracey, please," she interrupted, laughing. "Mrs. Parrish makes me feel so old."

"Tracey it is," he said. "Now, let's get these tryouts underway! We're going to start with a little warmup, jogging a few laps around the gym, some stretching and then we'll get some drills going. Sound good?"

He didn't wait for a response before continuing.

"Three laps around the gym, then come back to the center circle."

The herd of girls took off in a jog, and Cora was slow to follow. She counted their heads as they bobbed around the gym floor. Twenty-three girls. She watched as Sophie and her friends quickly accelerated to the front of the pack.

Cora wasn't surprised. Of all the girls at tryouts, Sophie and her gang looked the most prepared.

Cora spotted a few girls dressed like her, in their school shirts and shoes.

She watched as Sophie and her three friends crept ahead of the group. Coach Parrish wheeled a cart full of balls to the center of the gym, his clipboard close by. At the start of the second lap, a sharp pain pinched Cora's side.

How can I make it through tryouts if I'm already struggling? she wondered.

Keep going, she told herself. She focused on each step, putting one foot in front of the other. She counted her steps and focused on her shoes, anything to keep the attention from the pain in her side. She looked up, measuring her progress.

Sophie and Danika surged ahead, a wide gap broadening between them and their two friends. Addie and Chloe lagged behind them, and behind them, a large majority of the girls. She was still last, but a few girls had fallen behind, within reaching distance of Cora. She focused on her steps. One foot in front of the other, over and over and over again. She passed one girl, and then another. Cora was delighted she wasn't dead last. She completed her second lap, and invigorated by her progress, tried to increase her speed, but the pain in her side slowed her down. Sophie and Danika were already coming to the center of the court, hands on their hips, catching their breath.

Just finish, she told herself. *Focus on the next step.* Cora thought of that first visit with Max, scaling the waterfall. How much fear had gripped her, and yet, she had done it. She had scaled the wall and made it to the top. She thought of the glowworm cave, and how she had been brave and how the payoff had been huge.

Cora made a mental list of the things she had accomplished, even in her dreams, and by the end of the warmup laps, her confidence rose.

She rounded the last corner of her third lap and jogged to the center of the court, where the rest of the girls stretched on the ground, reaching for their toes.

Cora picked a spot near Sophie, who smiled encouragingly.

Coach Parrish waited for the last two girls to join and led them in a few quick stretches.

"Okay," he said, clapping his hands together. "Now that we're warm, we're going to get going with some basic drills. Who has played volleyball before?" A few hands shot up, and he glanced around the room.

"Right. I want everyone to partner up." He counted quickly. "There's an odd number, so whoever is left over can partner with Tracey."

Tracey smiled and gave a small wave.

A soft murmur ran through the girls as they all found partners. Cora flushed. She hated finding a partner when Mia wasn't around.

"Cora?" She heard a voice and turned slightly. It was Sophie. "Want to be my partner?" Cora smiled, relieved that Sophie asked to be her partner.

"Once you've found your partner, stand across from each other. The first thing we're going to work on is passing." Coach Parrish tossed a volleyball from one hand to the other as he walked down the line of girls, making sure everyone had a partner. Tracey and her partner stood at the end of the line.

"A pass is usually the first and most common way to hit a volleyball," Coach Parrish explained. "When someone serves the ball to your side of the court, this is the way you will receive the serve." He held his arms out, and folding his hands together, his thumbs touching, his forearms straight and together, creating a straight plane. His knees had a slight bend and he demonstrated passing the volleyball.

"Keep your arms straight and don't swing them." He made an exaggerated swing with his arms. "If you need to move them up or down, use your knees."

The two lines of girls extended their arms, practicing their form. Coach Parrish walked by, checking to make sure everyone's passing stance looked right.

"Remember to keep your thumbs uncrossed," he called to the group as he watched. "Good, good," he said as he went down the line, nearing Cora.

"Looks good," he said, glancing at her arms. "Now let's go ahead and toss the ball to our partner. We'll practice passing for a while."

Balls soared through the air as partners lobbed balls to each other.

"Ready?" Sophie asked, picking up a ball at her feet.

Cora nodded, focused intently on keeping her thumbs together, her forearms straight. Sophie tossed the ball and Cora watched it arc in the air, coming towards her. She moved her arms, following the ball's trajectory. It skimmed her forearm and shot to the side. Sophie ran after the ball and Cora's face flushed with embarrassment.

"Sorry!" Cora called.

"Good try!" Sophie said, returning with the ball. "Want to try again?"

Cora shook her head. "It's your turn!"

Sophie tossed the ball over, and Cora was relieved she caught it. She tossed the ball to Sophie. Sophie squared her legs, bent her knees, and watched the ball soar through the air. It landed on Sophie's extended forearms and arced beautifully in the air.

"Nice job," Coach Parrish exclaimed as he walked past. "Cora, are you getting the hang of it?"

Cora smiled sheepishly and attempted a nod. It was her turn.

Sophie threw the ball softly, and Cora watched again. It was going to her left, and she shuffled her feet, careful to keep her forearms level. The ball landed with a sting, but bounced straight off her arm, into the air.

"Excellent!" Coach Parrish said. "Nice job, you two."

Cora couldn't contain her excitement, a wide grin forming on her face.

"Good job!" Sophie said, excitedly.

"Thanks!" Cora said, and for the first time since the tryout started, she felt genuine enthusiasm.

They practiced passing and a few other drills before Coach Parrish blew a whistle and herded them all back to the middle of the court. Cora glanced at the clock. It was almost five. Cora was surprised time passed so quickly.

"Good job today," he said, his hands clasped together. "I saw a lot of good things. Tomorrow, same time. We won't have answers as to who made the team by tomorrow, but by the end of this week we'll know, okay?"

The girls nodded in agreement.

"See you tomorrow then!"

"Hey, Cora," Sophie called, as Cora stood to leave. "Good job today."

"Thanks, Sophie." Cora replied, smiling. "You did a good job, too."

Cora pushed open the heavy doors out of the gym, and for the first time felt a genuine sense of belonging.

Chapter 38

"WELL? HOW WAS IT?" Julie asked when Cora opened the door to the car.

Cora looked at her, a wide smile plastered across her face.

"Mom, it was actually so fun. I met a girl there who was so nice. Sophie," Cora went on. "She asked to be my partner for the first drill, and then we were partners for the rest of tryouts."

"Oh honey, I'm so glad to hear you had a good time." Her mom sounded relieved. "Sophie does sound very nice. Have you seen her at school before?"

Julie put the car in drive and pulled away from the school parking lot.

Cora shook her head. "No, I've never seen her."

"What did you think of the coach? Was the coach nice?"

"Yeah. Coach Parrish? I think that was his name. But yeah, he was nice. I was late at first and he kind of yelled, but after that he was nice."

"Well, it sounds like you had a really great first day," Julie said.

"It was a lot better than I was expecting. And the drills were even kind of fun," Cora said. "We go back tomorrow, and then the coach said we would find out in the next few days who made the team."

Julie nodded. "That's great, sweetie! I'm really proud of you for trying out." She patted Cora's knee. "Oh," she said, handing Cora her phone. "Mia called while you were at tryouts, and she wants you to call her when you're done."

Cora dialed the number for Mia's mom and listened to the ring. Mia answered after the first ring.

"Cora! Hi!" Mia's voice was happy, ringing through the phone.

"Hi, Mia!" Cora replied. Normally she had to consciously try to match Mia's excitement, but today it was genuine.

"I was just wondering how tryouts went," Mia said.

"It was really fun," Cora said. She fiddled with the hem on her shorts as she spoke. "I spent all day worrying about it, and in the end, it was a lot of fun."

"Did you know anyone else there?" Mia asked. In the background, Cora heard Mia's mom telling her it was time for dinner.

"Not really. There were some girls I recognized but no one that I really knew," Cora explained. "But one girl was super nice, Sophie."

"Oh, Sophie King?" Mia asked. She didn't wait for Cora to respond. "Sophie King is in one of my classes. She is really nice."

"Maybe? I'm not sure what her last name is."

"I'm sorry this was so fast, but my mom needs my help. I just wanted to see how it went today."

"Thanks, Mia! That was really nice of you. I'll see you tomorrow!" Cora pulled the phone from her ear and hit the red X, ending the call.

She handed the phone to her mom, who dropped it in the empty cup holder.

"Well, day one is done, and only one more to go," Julie said. "Hopefully tomorrow won't be as stressful waiting. Sometimes the anticipation is the worst part."

Cora nodded in agreement. *The longer you wait, the bigger it gets,* she thought.

Her mom pulled into the garage and turned the car off.

"Are you starving?" she asked, grabbing Cora's backpack from the backseat. "I'll get this."

Cora hadn't realized how hungry she was, but she was suddenly ravenous.

"Yes!" She exclaimed.

Her mom laughed. "I thought that might be the case. I made chicken and rice casserole, the one you like," she said with a wink.

"Dad's home already?" She asked.

Her mom nodded. "Yep, he came home a little early today."

She opened the garage door and a wave of warm kitchen air greeted her. The smell of dinner cooking made Cora's mouth water.

"The casserole should be almost done," her mom said. She walked into the kitchen, pulled open the oven door and pulled a piece of foil off the casserole dish. "Five more minutes," she smiled at Cora.

"Cora!" A voice boomed from behind her, and Cora turned to see her dad rounding the corner. "How was it? I've been thinking of you all day!" He folded her into a giant hug.

"It was good," Cora said, her voice muffled, lost in the cocoon of his embrace. He held her like that, wrapped up tight, for a few moments before releasing her.

"I'm sorry, I couldn't hear you," he smiled. "How was it?"

Cora laughed. "It was good! The coach was nice, I met a girl there and we were partners for most of it." She shrugged. "We go back tomorrow."

Her dad held up his hand, waiting for a high five.

"Cora, that is awesome," he said, emphasizing each word. "I'm really proud of you."

"Thanks," Cora said, a little sheepishly. Cora didn't like all the attention on her, but her parent's reactions bolstered her.

"Will you go get Reagan?" her mom asked, looking over Cora's head at her dad. "Dinner is ready."

Her dad saluted and turned on his heel. Her mom shook her head, chuckling. For a fleeting moment, things were almost normal. Almost.

Chapter 39

A SWIFT KNOCK RUSTLED Reagan from her cocoon in her bed. By the knock, she could tell it was her dad.

"Reagan? It's time for dinner," he said, softly.

"I'm not hungry," Reagan mumbled. She made her voice sound groggy, hoping he would let her stay in her room.

"Well come sit at the table then. You don't have to eat if you're not hungry, but you do need to come downstairs."

She groaned and threw the covers off her body. She had rifled through Max's room all morning, rummaging through drawers and piles of paper, searching for some sign of the compass, but without any luck. Defeated, she'd returned to her bedroom lair where she spent the afternoon sulking.

"There she is!" he said, opening his arms wide for an embrace.

Reagan stood, waiting for him to put his arms down so she could pass. She crossed her arms on her chest. Reluctantly, he dropped them.

"Cora had her tryouts today," he said. "Why don't you ask her how they went?"

Reagan rolled her eyes and nodded, even though she truly could not care any less how Cora's dumb volleyball tryouts went. Not only was she only in sixth grade, but she had literally never touched a volleyball in her life. *If Cora managed to make the team, that coach must be seriously deranged,* Reagan thought.

She followed her dad down the stairs, ignoring his questions and feeling grumpier than usual at his generally happy mood.

She sat at the kitchen table, noted it was set for four. A tug of sadness pulled at her heart and she looked away from the place where Max usually sat. Spending so much time amidst his things had made her especially sentimental and sad.

"Hey, sweetie," her mom said, placing a steaming plate of what looked like chicken and rice casserole in front of her.

"Hi," Reagan grumbled.

A feeling of regret swept through her body at her curt reply to her mom.

Cora sat at the table, her gaze avoiding Reagan's. Something about Cora was different, but Reagan couldn't put her finger on it. She still had that wild, frizzy red hair, but it was pulled back in a ponytail. Instead of her usual jeans, she was wearing those mint green athletic shorts they purchased the day before. Reagan studied Cora from across the table. It wasn't a physical change, she finally decided. But her movements were lighter, maybe. Cora always reminded Reagan of a baby deer, awkward and unstable on new legs. But tonight, Cora's countenance was more confident. Like she was more comfortable in her own body.

Reagan seized the opportunity to knock Cora's confidence down again.

"How were volleyball tryouts?" Reagan asked, reaching for a slice of homemade bread her mom had set on the table.

Cora's eyes met Reagan's, and Reagan could tell Cora was debating how to answer. It was out of character for Reagan to take any interest in Cora's life, and from the look in Cora's face, she was skeptical.

"They were good," Cora answered evasively.

"Did you make the team?" Reagan asked.

Cora buttered a piece of bread as she answered. "We go back tomorrow for more tryouts, and then we'll find out a few days later."

"Even if she doesn't make it," Ned interrupted, pulling his chair from the table. "The important thing is that you tried. That you showed up and worked your hardest." He smiled at Cora. "Right, Cor?"

Reagan scoffed and three sets of eyes turned to look at her.

"Right, that's the most important thing," she said sarcastically, rolling her eyes.

"Reagan," her mom said, a warning in her voice. "That *is* the most important thing."

"Besides, how could she not make it?" Ned said, loudly. "They'd be missing out if they didn't want Miss Cora on the team!"

Across the table, Cora's cheeks flushed a crimson red.

The rest of dinner passed and Reagan tuned out of the casual conversation around her, eventually slinking back upstairs to her room. It seemed like she was always counting down the minutes until she could retreat to her room again. To bury herself underneath the covers. She forgot what it was like to feel anything but the suffocating pain and the waves of anger that coursed through her body like giant swells. She was stuck in a dark loop, and if she wasn't sure if she didn't care enough to get herself out, or if the thought of getting herself out was so overwhelming, she didn't know where to start.

Reagan imagined herself sprawled in the depths of an illusory maze. It was an easy descent, and now the hard part lay ahead of her. Getting out. If she actually could. If she actually wanted to.

It was a lonely experience, being a bereaved sibling. Reagan had spent hours wading through information, looking for answers. Connection. Someone that had endured the heartbreak and was still standing, perhaps.

It was hard to get a handle on her emotions, and they fluctuated within her. She imagined the emotions in different colors, coursing through her veins. Guilt was purple, anger was red, and anxiety was green, like a virus attacking her system. Sadness was blue.

She imagined the colors filling her veins like a subway map, highlighting the various routes. Reagan had gone to New York City years ago for a soccer camp. Her team stayed in a college dorm and took the subway to the collegiate soccer field they were playing. She had studied the subway map, following the yellow line with her finger, mapping her route. She imagined the same lines in her body, mapping out the course of all the emotions running inside her.

Her eyelids drooped. Her dreams were sometimes haunted by Max, by happy memories of him, and she would wake feeling like the dream was her reality. And then she would come to remember that, to her heart's dismay, her dream was just that, a dream. She closed her eyes, thinking that being awake was just as much as of a nightmare as the dreams that haunted her sleep.

Chapter 40

CORA SCROLLED AIMLESSLY WITH the trackpad on her family's computer, her fingers flicking upward. She didn't know what she was looking for; she hoped an image would jump out at her. She was hoping Max would somehow communicate with her, let her know where to meet him.

"Finding anything good?" A voice startled her, and she turned to see her dad leaning on the door frame, his arms crossed in front of him.

She shrugged and guilt washed over her, like she had been caught doing something she shouldn't have been.

"What are you looking for? Anything in particular?" he asked from the doorway.

Cora shrugged again.

"I don't really know. Just something to draw, I guess," she said, turning back to the computer.

"Mind if I join you?"

Cora shook her head, even though she preferred to be alone. She felt an obligation, a sense of duty to include her parents in her life, even in the smallest ways. Like looking at locations on the internet.

Her dad pulled a chair up next to the computer, and sat on it backwards, his chin propped on his hands.

"I've noticed you're drawing a lot of landscapes lately," her dad said, keeping his eyes on the computer screen.

"Yeah, I guess. They've just been fun to draw," she said.

"Makes sense," he said, nodding slowly. "You know, it's good to have a release. To have some sort of escape. It seems like drawing may be that for you, and I'm glad you have that."

You have no idea what kind of escape it is, Cora thought. She avoided eye contact, worried that her eyes might give her secret away.

"Dad?" She asked quietly. "What do you think happens to us when we die?" She didn't finish the question, what she really wanted to know. *Where is Max now?*

Her dad blew out a stream of air next to her and took a deep breath before responding.

"You know, sweetie, I don't think anyone really knows. But I do believe Max is somewhere carefree, totally healthy and healed from the afflictions he faced here." His voice cracked, and he coughed to cover the emotion creeping into his voice. "Have you heard about the legend of a Phoenix?"

Cora shook her head, blinking back tears. Ned cleared this throat before continuing.

"Ancient cultures believed in a mythical bird, the Phoenix. Supposedly, it was a beautiful creature that would set itself on fire. A new Phoenix is born from the ashes, destined to live another, wonderful life." He paused, and Cora was silent, waiting for him to continue.

"I like to think of Max as a Phoenix, being reborn. Rising from the ashes in a new, refined version of himself. I have to believe that. I have to believe we'll see him again. Otherwise, it's just too much."

Cora nodded as tears welled in her eyes. The last thing she wanted to do was cry in the office with her dad. She blinked the tears back and kept scrolling. She picked the first image her eyes landed on, desperate to move the conversation forward.

"What about this one?" she asked, pointing to a wintery scene with lush green pine trees and a white blanket of snow. The sky was a bright blue, and Cora could almost feel the cool, crisp air on her skin through the computer screen.

"Beautiful," her dad said. "I haven't seen you draw anything like that, it'll be fun to see what you come up with."

Part of her wanted to spill her secret right then, to ease some of the ache she saw in her dad's eyes. But she knew she couldn't—or wouldn't. She wasn't sure which one.

She wasn't sure what the rules were of that post-mortal world, and she didn't want to jeopardize her chance to be with Max.

She yawned. "Thanks, Dad," she said. "I'm tired though. I'm not sure I'm going to draw anything tonight." It was one of the only times she had ever lied to him, and she was sure he could see right through it.

"I bet," he said, sympathetically. "A day of volleyball tryouts will do that to you." He pulled her close and kissed the top of her head.

"I'm going to go upstairs and see if I have any homework I need to take care of." It was her second lie of the night.

"Okay, Cor-bug," her dad said kindly. "If you need any help, you know where to find me." He smiled again and stood, putting his chair back in the corner of the room. He followed Cora out the door, switching off the light as they left.

"Good luck," he told her, giving her a side squeeze. "We'll be up in a bit to check on you."

Cora hurried up the stairs, tiptoeing past Reagan's room. It was a habit now, muscle memory to glide past her room unnoticed.

She paused outside her door, looking at the empty room at the end of the hall. There was always a dull ache in her heart, but sometimes, some things made it worse, like looking at Max's empty room.

She was just about to open her door when she realized she forgot her backpack downstairs.

Cora crept down the stairs, hoping to grab her bag and scurry back upstairs, unnoticed. She could only imagine the wrath she would face if she managed to disturb Reagan.

She heard her parents muffled voices growing clearer as she got closer.

"I just don't know. I don't know what to do," her mom said, over the splatter of the kitchen sink.

"I don't know that there is anything we can do," her dad said. "She's almost an adult, Julie. She's going to do whatever she wants."

"I know, but she can't spend all day every day in her room, Ned," her mom said, desperation in her voice. "I'm worried about her. Really worried. I asked her if she wanted to see a professional and she didn't say no. Maybe I should ask her again."

Cora backed up, quietly grabbed her backpack, and retreated upstairs.

Once in her room, she unzipped her bag, pulling out her jeans and books and sketchpad. She quickly scanned her notebooks, checking for homework. She was relieved that there wasn't any. She stacked her school supplies in a neat corner on her desk and repacked her backpack for the following day. She wanted to shower, and then get to drawing.

She plucked her towel from the hook on the back of her door and hurried into the bathroom, closing the door behind her. The hot water hit her body, and it felt good. Her muscles were sore already, her forearms tender from hitting the volleyball so many times. But a new sense of satisfaction filled her, a sense of accomplishment that she hadn't felt in a long time. The water pummeled her back, and she suddenly a wave of exhaustion overcame her. She turned the water off and wrapped herself in a towel. Squeezing a glob of toothpaste on her toothbrush, she finally looked at herself in the mirror.

There was something about herself that she didn't quite recognize, something she couldn't put her finger on. She held her own gaze, something she had never done before. Normally when she looked in the mirror, she averted her eyes as quickly as possible, avoiding the face staring back at her. But now, she saw something new within the eyes staring back at her.

She remembered something her dad had told her a few nights ago—that you believe what you tell yourself.

"You are brave. You are good at volleyball. You are going to make the volleyball team," she whispered to the girl in the mirror. She didn't feel anything different. She raised her voice, tried again.

"You are brave. You are good at volleyball. You are going to make the volleyball team." The corners of her mouth twitched with a small smile. She raised her voice again.

"You are brave. You are good at volleyball. You are going to make the volleyball team!"

"You are also very weird, and I need to brush my teeth," a voice from outside the door interrupted her, and Cora jumped. Reagan. Of all people, of all things for her to overhear, why did it have to be when Cora was literally talking to herself?

She wrapped the towel tighter and kept her eyes down as she pulled open the bathroom door.

Reagan stood blocking the doorway. She didn't budge when Cora opened the door, and Cora was forced to skirt around her. She couldn't bear to meet Reagan's gaze, which she knew was fixed on her. Her eyes caught hold of something yellow, the bracelet Cora made for her, dangling from Reagan's wrist. Cora was momentarily stunned.

"That was really something," Reagan said sardonically. "You know, that positive self-talk stuff only works if you actually have the skills to back it up. So, don't count on your little mantras doing you any favors." She shrugged and closed the bathroom door behind her.

Cora hesitated outside her bedroom for a moment, watching the closed bathroom door. Reagan was insufferable. Indignant anger surged inside Cora, before remembering Max's caution about Reagan. *I think she's struggling more than anyone realizes.*

The anger inside Cora dissipated, replaced instead by an aching sadness for her older sister. Inside her room, she quickly changed into her pajamas, and settled into her usual spot on the floor for her nightly sketching session, snatching the compass necklace from its safe spot on her desk. She smoothed the printout of the winter forest on the floor next to her and slipped the necklace over her head. Cora rubbed the compass between her thumb and forefinger, regarding every detail of the metal underneath her fingertips. Then she slipped on her shoes, just in case she needed them on her next adventure.

She was ready. Cora picked up her pencil and held it lightly in her hand. She drew soft lines, sketching the outlines of the forest. As her arm moved, Cora's muscles ached all over her body, in places she didn't know muscles existed. Her eyelids were heavy already, and she strained to keep them open, until she finally succumbed and fell into a deep, heavy sleep.

Chapter 41

REAGAN REPLAYED THE SCENE from the bathroom over and over in her mind. *Seriously, what loser talks to themselves*, she thought. Remembering her harsh words made Reagan feel a strange sense of satisfaction. Reagan didn't try to hide the fact that she disliked Cora, but it went deeper than that. Deep within Reagan lived a dark secret that she really wished it would have been Cora, not Max, who had died. Punishing Cora with cruel comments and mean stares was Reagan's vindication, her way of getting back at Cora for being alive.

She patiently waited for the house to quiet. Her breath was steady, her heart beating calmly. This was the most serenity Reagan had experienced in a long time, and her plan was simple: find Max's compass. She tried to tell herself her motivation for finding the compass was altruistic, that she wanted to give her mom a memento of her late brother, but Reagan also had a darker motivation.

She was hopeful that the compass would distract her mother enough that Reagan could slip deeper into the dark oblivion until one day, she could just disappear.

Reagan would have never described herself as suicidal. No, that was reserved for the kids who were bullied, who dyed their hair dark and listened to sad, screaming songs. It wasn't for the star athlete, the most popular girl in school. The girl who had hordes of friends, and boyfriends in waiting. Yet, here she was with suicidal ideations replaying on a constant loop in her mind.

She wanted to scream at them that they had no idea, that it could happen to them or their family, too. You never know until you know.

She threw the covers from her body and crept out of her room, down the hallway. Cora's light had been on surprisingly late, but it was now switched off. She stopped at Max's door, bracing herself with a deep breath. She twisted the doorknob and the door swung open.

The air smelled faintly like him, and Reagan was momentarily stunned, standing in his room amidst his things. She cringed, as if she were committing an act of betrayal, rifling through his belongings. But, she told herself, this was a token for her mom.

She took another deep breath, steeling herself, and opened his closet door. His shirts and jackets hung neatly in front of her, sweaters were folded on the shelf. His pants and jeans were hung, and Reagan was surprised by how the mere sight of Max's clothes completely unraveled her. She swallowed hard and willed herself not to cry. *Get to work, Reagan,* she told herself harshly. She reached for the pants, hung neatly in half. She checked the pockets, disappointed when she came up empty handed. Pocket after pocket she searched, finding nothing.

She moved onto the sweatshirts and hoodies, checking each pocket meticulously.

She moved to his desk, quietly opening drawers and overturning notebooks and books, searching for the golden compass.

It has to be here somewhere, she thought. *Where is it?*

She straightened and rested her hands on her hips, trying to think like Max. She spotted the nightstand next to his bed and hurried over. Books were neatly stacked inside, and a pad of yellow sticky notes. A note was scribbled in Max's messy scrawl on the top note: *What would you do if you had no fear?*

Reagan sat on the edge of the bed, defeated, and holding the sticky note in her hand. When she saw the ink on the yellow note, she hoped it would be a clue, some sort of beacon leading her to the compass. But it was just some inspirational quote from Max.

The compass wasn't in Max's room. Julie had searched, and Reagan had scoured and neither found the compass. Defeated and exhausted, Reagan dragged herself back to down the hall to her own bedroom.

At the door of her room, she paused, staring at the closed door of her parents' room. She felt like she had let her mom down once again. A small part of her wanted to crawl in next to her mom in bed. She wanted to cry and feel her mom's loving embrace around her, telling her it would all be okay. But that sort of thing only worked when you were little, when you're young enough to believe everything you hear.

Reagan was old enough to know better, to know that there was no way everything would be okay. She knew it would just take one step, one foot in front of the other and saying those three words—I need help—and her parents would do anything they could. But that step, no matter how small, was an insurmountable step Reagan just couldn't bring herself to take.

She opened the door to her bedroom, welcomed by the familiar darkness.

Before she succumbed to sleep, Reagan had a sneaking thought that one person in the house might know where the compass was: Cora. Tomorrow, she would ransack Cora's room until she found it.

Chapter 42

JULIE'S PHONE BUZZED FROM the center console and Julie fumbled to answer on her Bluetooth. Cora sat in the passenger seat, feeling a new excitement about school and volleyball tryouts.

"Hello?" Julie answered.

"Hello, is Mrs. Jones available?" The voice on the other end of the call was polite, but clipped.

"This is she. May I ask who is calling?" Julie asked. She flicked on her blinker and turned into the school parking lot.

"Yes, Mrs. Jones, this is Mrs. Ayers, the attendance counselor at Rolling Hills High School."

"Okay," Julie said slowly. "How can I help you today, Mrs. Ayers?"

"Well, Mrs. Jones, I've been reviewing your daughter Reagan's attendance record, and I'm afraid to tell you that she's been absent for twenty consecutive days. Our graduation policy clearly states that any student who misses twenty-one days won't be able to participate in high school graduation."

"I'm sorry, what?" Julie asked, confused. "I'm not totally clear on what you're saying. Reagan hasn't been to school, no. But I didn't think she had classes to be there for?"

"Well, unfortunately, that's not entirely true, Mrs. Jones."

Julie inched the car forward. They were in the drop-off line, waiting for Cora's turn to hop out. Cora hoped the line would slow down so she could hear the end of the conversation, so she could be privy to whatever was happening in Reagan's life.

"I'm sorry, I don't think I am understanding correctly," Julie said. "So, Reagan has in-person classes she's supposed to be there for?"

"Yes, that is correct," came the terse reply. "And like I said, Reagan has missed twenty consecutive days, which means one more absence and she won't be eligible for graduation."

"Is today day twenty or twenty-one?" Julie asked. The drop-off line crept forward, and Julie released the brake. The car crawled forward one spot.

"Today is day twenty. We always give a warning call to parents before the twenty-first day,"

"Mrs. Ayers, I'm sure you know that Reagan is going through a difficult time right now," Julie said. "Is there some leeway for students who experience a death in the family or other traumatic event?"

"Unfortunately, no, there is no leeway." Mrs. Ayers' voice was flat, void of any emotion.

"So, Reagan just has to come to school today or tomorrow, is that right?" Julie clarified.

"Well, yes," Mrs. Ayers said.

"And if those absences are excused, does that still count against her?" Julie asked.

"Well, no. If they're excused absences, they won't count against the attendance policy."

Cora cast a sideways glance at Julie, and noticed a small, triumphant smile on her face.

"Thank you for the call, Mrs. Ayers," she said. "I will send a note with Reagan tomorrow. Have a nice day."

She ended the call without waiting for a response.

"Thanks for the ride, mom," Cora said, snapping Julie out of her trance.

"Wait! Good luck today." Julie planted a quick kiss on Cora's cheek. "Love you, sweetie."

Cora smiled and mouthed, "Love you too," as she slammed the car door shut.

Chapter 43

REAGAN SHOT OUT OF bed the second she heard the garage door close. She had limited time before her mom returned from dropping Cora off at school. She threw on a sweatshirt, hurried down the hall to Cora's room, and opened the door. Even though she was eleven, Cora's room still looked like a child's. Something about the pale pinks and soft tones made Reagan feel like she was in a little girl's fairy tale. Reagan stood in the doorway, looking at the framed pictures of Cora and Mia strewn on the shelves. A brief flash of blazing-hot jealousy coursed through Reagan. Their friendship was so genuine, so real. Reagan always pitied Cora for only having a single friend, for being so anti-social that she only managed to make one friend in her years of schooling. And now she found herself slightly jealous. She looked away from the pictures, focusing on her task at hand.

She pulled open the drawer to the nightstand, shuffling papers and a magazine around so she could see the inside. There was no compass, but she did find Cora's journal. She flipped the pages open, reading through the mundane details of her little sister's life. She read Cora's scrawl about the fun things she did with Mia, about things that happened at school. There was a long pause in the journal and Reagan instinctively knew it was the days or weeks or months after Max died. The journal picked back up with a strange entry reading.

I had a really weird dream about Max. We were in some sort of jungle with a giant waterfall, and he jumped into the water below. I had to follow him, but in the dream, I lost his compass. We had to find it, and as soon as we did, I woke up. But the weird thing is that when I woke up, my shoes were totally wet.

The entry stopped, and Reagan froze. The compass. The wet shoes. The nighttime shower that left the tub filled with red sand. Reagan's breath quickened and she flipped the page. *Another dream last night,* Cora confided to her journal. *This time we were in a slot canyon. Same thing with the compass. It was in my pocket and then it started to slip out. I caught it, and as soon as I did, I woke up. But my shoes were filled with red sand, and I had sand all over my body. These dreams feel so real. I'm not sure what's happening. Max is always there, though. I don't want the dreams to end.*

Reagan couldn't pull her eyes from the journal. She knew the compass had to be here somewhere. And based on Cora's dreams, it wasn't just an ordinary compass. Reagan was desperate to read more. She flipped the pages and read voraciously, reading about a glow worm cave in New Zealand, and then a faraway desert. She shook her head. She couldn't really be seeing Max, could she?

Reagan kept reading. After the last dream entry, there was one more dated from that day.

Ideas to help Reagan:

Reagan's vision blurred with tears. Nothing had been added to her idea list yet. Reagan wanted there to be more, she wanted to read about how Cora intended to help her. As she sat looking at the blank page, even she couldn't come up with ways to help herself.

It's too late, Cora, she thought.

She held the book in her hands, fitting in the crook of her palms. She set the journal gently back in the nightstand drawer. She wondered what Cora would write tonight, what ideas she would come up with. She wondered if Cora would take a long break from writing after Reagan was gone, if the pages would remain blank for months. She wondered if Cora would will herself to dream about her the way she dreamed about Max.

Lost in thought, Reagan didn't hear the sound of the garage door opening. She didn't hear the footsteps coming up the stairs.

"Reagan?" Her mom's voice pulled her from her abysmal thoughts. "Sweetie, what are you doing in here?"

Reagan was sitting on the edge of Cora's bed, and she looked at her mom, surprised.

"Mom! I was just looking for something," Reagan said, honestly.

Her mom squinted. "What were you looking for?"

"Cora's bead kit," Reagan lied. "She made me a bracelet and I wanted to make her one in return."

"Oh," her mom said, glancing around the room. "I'm sure it's around here somewhere."

Her eyes floated to the back corner of the desk, where a transparent pink box sat.

"There it is," her mom said.

Reagan followed her mom's gaze, and there, on the desk, something else caught her eye. A small, blue, heart-shaped trinket box. She wanted to run to it, to pull off the lid and peer inside. Instinctively, she knew the compass would be in there.

Her mom crossed the room and grabbed the bead box. "Let's go downstairs," she said. "You can make the bracelet while I clean up the kitchen."

She extended a hand to Reagan, helping her up off the bed.

Reagan stood. She was annoyed the hunt for the compass would have to wait, but she couldn't risk searching for it with her mom around.

"Any homework or school work today?" her mom asked as she piled dishes in the sink.

"Not really," Reagan mumbled, stringing beads onto a thin strand of elastic.

Julie paused before continuing.

"Mrs. Ayers from the school called this morning. She said you're at risk of not graduating." She paused, but Reagan had nothing to say.

"We have to take a note into the school to excuse the absences today," she continued. She was standing at the sink, rinsing dishes and filling the French toast bowl with hot, soapy water. "Why don't you go upstairs and get changed? We could run to the school, maybe run a few errands. We could go to lunch and then you could pick Cora up from volleyball tryouts with me."

"I actually thought I would just go back upstairs," Reagan said flatly. *And stay upstairs,* she thought.

"I think some fresh air would be nice," Julie said, meeting Reagan's eyes. They held eye contact, a silent battle. Reagan broke first.

"I'll go shower," she said, sliding off the barstool.

Reagan stood in the bathroom mirror. The reflection staring back at her was unrecognizable. Her mass of blond hair sat in a tangle on the top of her head. Dark, half-moon circles hung below her eyes. Her cheeks were sunken, withdrawn. Her features hadn't changed, but there was no light behind her eyes, no vigor to her face. Her skin looked dull, ashen. She had avoided eye contact with herself every time she was in the bathroom, and her reflection took her breath away.

She stood under the water, incrementally turning the water hotter and hotter until she nearly couldn't stand it. The water stung as it hit her shoulders, and she let it pummel her back and shoulders, let the water burn on her skin, as if it was her punishment, her moment of reckoning for all of her ill thoughts towards her family, towards Cora, even towards Max. She stood under the steady stream of the shower until the sting disappeared. She dipped her head back into the water, feeling the water touch her scalp. It was cathartic, in a way, releasing all of her energy into the steam to be evaporated, floating freely above her and vanishing in the pale bathroom light.

When she was done, she stood in front of the mirror again. Her skin was red, splotchy from the scrubbing and hot water. She knew what to expect in her reflection this time, and it didn't surprise her like it did before. But she still looked at that girl like a stranger. How odd, she thought, to be a stranger within your own body. To look in the mirror, and stare back at an unknown reflection.

It wasn't just the physical changes she didn't recognize, she realized, still staring at herself. She didn't recognize what was deep within her; she didn't recognize her soul. She was unable to look at herself anymore, to face herself.

She turned from the mirror, flipped off the bathroom light, and hurried into her room to change.

Chapter 44

WHEN THE END-OF-DAY BELL rang, Cora shuffled her papers into her binder, stacked her books, and hustled out of the classroom. Cora had been anxious all day, but it wasn't the same nervous energy she experienced the day before. This was excited anticipation.

She found Mia at her locker. "I just wanted to say bye. I have to go get changed for volleyball tryouts," she said breathlessly.

"Good luck!" Mia said. "You're going to do awesome!" She pulled Cora in for a hug.

Cora made her way to her locker, deftly spinning the lock to open without a hitch. She grabbed her backpack and pulled out her athletic shorts. She had a hair tie around her wrist—she'd remembered that this time. She carefully filled her backpack with the notebooks and textbooks she needed for that night and hoisted it into the locker.

Locked in her stall in the bathroom, she heard the door open, and a herd of girls enter. They were mid-conversation, peals of laughter filling room. When the echo subsided, Cora heard one of the girls call out.

"Soph, are you going to partner with your BFF again today?" she asked.

"Yeah, like, was that your random act of kindness for the day or what? Or did you feel bad for her because, well... you know," another girl asked.

"Guys, don't be mean," came a defending voice. "She's just weird, okay? And her freaking brother died, so like, let's not be total jerks."

Cora's face flushed. There was no question who they were talking about. She didn't want to stay in the stall and face more of their criticism, but she couldn't open the door and face them. She was mortified.

"Yeah, guys, come on," said Sophie. "I thought it was really cool of her. It would be so hard to try out totally by yourself. Besides, she's really nice and she was actually kind of good by the end."

"Who cares if she's good? She's just so awkward." There it was—the word that had haunted her for as long as she could remember. "Does she have any friends?"

Tears stung Cora's eyes. She was trapped, and the last thing she wanted to do, the last thing she could physically do, was walk into the gym with these girls and pretend she was okay. She lingered in the bathroom, weighing her options. Suddenly, like a flash of inspiration, she remembered what Max had said about having just one second of bravery. *One second of being really, incredibly brave is all it takes,* she thought.

She took a deep breath, mustering all the courage in her being and flipped the lock, letting the door swing open. She took a step out. Two girls leaning against the bathroom counter stopped, their mouths open in wide Os.

Sophie was pulling up her socks and stopped as soon as she saw Cora's face. The fourth girl stopped lacing her shoes and watched.

A wave of panic surged through Cora, as all eyes stayed on her. She really hadn't thought through what she was going to say when she revealed herself, and now her tongue was tied.

"Cora," Sophie said, softly. "I, uh..."

The girls in front of the mirror averted their eyes, and Cora could tell by their body language they had been the ones talking about her.

"Maybe I am weird and awkward. I'm learning to love those things about myself because they make me, me. I don't want to be a girl who talks about other people in the bathroom. I'll take being weird and awkward over that."

She turned to leave but paused.

"Oh, and I do have one friend. Just one, but one is enough."

With a powerful thrust, she pushed open the bathroom door. She felt a force beside her and knew instinctively it was Max. She hadn't known that kind of strength, that bravery, existed in her, and her heart raced with exhilaration.

The door pushed open behind her, and footsteps followed.

"Cora," Sophie said, catching up to Cora at her locker. She was breathless. "I just wanted... I'm sorry," she said sheepishly. "I don't think you're weird or awkward. I think you're really nice. And I really didn't know anything about your brother, and I'm just really sorry."

Cora nodded, appreciating the apology. Sophie really hadn't said anything mean, but Cora was starting to see this was just how some people were. Some people built themselves up by tearing others down, and that wasn't something she wanted to be part of. She would rather build herself and Mia up on their own.

"Thanks," Cora said, finally.

"Are you going to stay for tryouts?" Sophie asked, her eyes hopeful.

"Yes," Cora said definitively. "I had fun yesterday, and I want to see where it goes today."

"I wasn't kidding when I said you were pretty good by the end of yesterday," Sophie said. "I meant it. Especially for never playing before." Cora wasn't sure if Sophie was trying to make her feel better, but she accepted the compliment.

"So, partners?" Sophie asked.

Cora smiled, but shook her head. "Thanks, but you can partner with one of your other friends. I think I'm going to partner with someone else."

Sophie nodded and glanced at the clock.

"Well, we should probably get to the gym. Tryouts start in a couple of minutes," she said, shifting her weight on her feet.

Cora closed her locker and the two walked side by side to the gym. Sophie's friends were huddled in the corner by the bathroom.

"Sorry, Cora," they mumbled sheepishly as Cora approached.

She smiled but didn't respond. An earlier version of herself would have hastily responded with comforting phrases to reassure them she was fine.

The truth was, she was fine. Those words had stung, but they were over. Those words didn't define her. She walked confidently into the gym, her eyes searching for someone to sit next to. They settled on a small blond girl. Cora recognized her as the girl who partnered with Tracey yesterday. She motioned to the space on the gym floor. "Is anyone sitting here?" she asked with a smile.

The girl looked at Cora, quickly shook her head, and averted her eyes.

Cora took a seat and leaned over. "I'm Cora," she said. "What's your name?"

"Sarah," the blonde said quietly, offering a shy smile to Cora before turning away again.

Cora saw a glimmer of recognition in that smile. A smile that was grateful to have a friend. Cora smiled to herself as Coach Parrish addressed the plan for tryouts. A few drills, a scrimmage, and then they would each talk with Coach Parrish, one on one, while the rest of the team worked on volleyball skills. She was working with Sarah on passing when she heard Coach Parrish call her name.

"Cora!" Coach Parrish's voice boomed across the gym. Cora turned, and he waved her over to a small office in the corner of the gym.

"So, Cora," he said, quickly checking his clipboard to make sure he got her name right. "You're in sixth grade?"

She nodded.

"Cool, cool," Coach Parrish continued. He flipped a page up on his clipboard, and Cora was nearly certain he was just stalling. "So, tell me about yourself. What sports have you played in the past?"

"None," Cora shook her head. "This is my first time trying out for anything."

"No sports at all?" He raised his eyebrows, surprised.

"No," Cora said, starting to feel self-conscious. "My older siblings played a little of everything, and my older sister is really good at soccer. I guess that gene just didn't get passed down to me."

"Well, I don't know about that," the coach said. "You exhibited real skill yesterday, even more so now that I know you've never really played before."

Cora was momentarily taken aback. This was the last thing she expected to hear come out of anyone's mouth, let alone someone who was keen at assessing athletic ability.

"And, more importantly, there were a few other attributes that I think will really add value to the team," he said. Cora couldn't believe her ears. *Will add value to the team?* "Yesterday, I really noticed that you never gave up. You were eager to learn and kept trying when you made a mistake. That's super important, and not just in volleyball."

Cora nodded, too shocked to say anything.

"The other thing I noticed," Coach Parrish continued, "was just how inclusive you were. I noticed you sitting by Sarah first thing today, and that is a sign of a truly great leader. Finding the people on the fringes and bringing them in. You know, you'll always have a friend that way."

He paused, and Cora looked at him.

"So, practices will be held a few times a week. We're just nailing down the dates and times, but we'll have that figured out for sure by next week. What other questions do you have for me?"

"Wait, so I made the team?" Cora asked, dumbfounded.

Coach Parrish tried to stifle a laugh.

"Yes, you made the team, Cora."

"But I thought we didn't find out right away?"

"Yeah, we usually tell people that just in case we need a few days to make a decision," he explained. "We didn't need much time for your decision. But some people won't find out until the end of tryouts when they meet with me, so just don't gloat about it, okay?"

"I won't at all," Cora said, shaking her head quickly. "So, do I stay, or am I done?"

"Nah, you can go ahead and get out of here," Coach Parrish said. "No need to stay. Be back here tomorrow at the same time, and we'll go over rules and expectations and all that good stuff. Have a good night, and see you tomorrow." He smiled as Cora stood, shaky on her legs.

"Thanks, and yeah, see you tomorrow."

Cora left the office, smiling and waving at Sarah before she left. Sarah smiled back before turning her attention to Tracey, who was on the other side of the gym, tossing her a ball.

Cora took it all in for a moment, trying to let Coach Parrish's words sink into her being. She sent a silent prayer to Max and closed her eyes, imagining him cheering for her.

She turned to leave the gym and pushed through the heavy doors, looking up at the clock on the wall. Tryouts didn't officially end for fifteen more minutes, which meant she had time to kill. She grabbed her backpack from her locker. She decided to wait outside for her mom. She walked out the doors and saw her mother's car already in the parking lot. She walked to the passenger side, feeling light, content, and maybe even happy.

She approached the car and noticed Reagan sitting in the passenger seat, and her mood shifted instantly. She sighed and pulled open the door to the backseat.

Reagan didn't say anything, just continued to stare at the phone in her lap.

"You're done early!" Her mom said, and Cora detected a bit of worry in her voice. "How did it go?"

Cora closed her eyes trying to make herself seem sad.

"Well," she said slowly, drawing out the last syllable as long as she could.

Her mom looked on expectantly. Reagan was poised to pretend like she wasn't listening, but Cora noticed her finger had stopped scrolling. Cora made her face as serious as possible.

"I made the team!" she exclaimed.

"What! Cora!" Her mom screamed and reached through the opening to the backseat to give Cora a one-armed hug. "I'm so proud of you!" She gave Cora a giant kiss on the side of her face.

"Thanks," Cora said, slightly embarrassed by all the attention.

"I'm actually shocked," Reagan said coolly from the front seat. Julie swatted her hand and gave her a small tsk sound. "You must have been like, their pity choice or something."

"Reagan, stop," her mom said quickly. "Cora, that is great news. So, what did they say?"

"Not too much, just that they'll figure practices and stuff out by next week. We have to go back tomorrow for team rules and that sort of thing," Cora explained.

"Did the coach say anything else?" her mom asked. She was turned, facing Cora her face alight with joy.

"He just said that he saw a natural athletic ability."

Reagan scoffed, interrupting Cora's story.

Cora and her mom ignored her. "And he liked that I was outgoing and nice to people."

"Are we talking about the same Cora?" Reagan asked.

Julie placed a gentle but firm hand on Reagan's leg and gave her a sharp shake of the head.

"Honey, that is great news. I'm so happy for you!" She smiled broadly.

Cora was happy for herself, too.

Chapter 45

IT TOOK EVERY OUNCE of willpower Reagan had not to say anything else about Cora making the volleyball team. It was completely preposterous, and the production that her mom made about Cora making the team was an absolute joke. She hated seeing Cora happy, hated seeing how enthusiastic her mom was about some lame intramural volleyball team.

So what, she made a middle-school sports team. Big deal. *Everyone that tried out probably made the team,* Reagan thought harshly.

Reagan won state championship soccer games, been selected for exclusive tournament play, she had even earned a full ride scholarship to a top soccer school. But she had also thrown all of that away.

She seethed silently, resentment festering. The pressure rose inside her, filling like a balloon about to burst. She imagined her fingers gripping a greased pole, her body dangling precariously over a dark ledge. It was a visual she had used as a crutch to evaluate how she was feeling. Especially dark days, she hung by just a finger or two. Other days, her four digits and thumb were grasped tightly. She formulated the image in her mind and made a mental note of the finger placement. She was holding on by a single finger and losing her grip quickly.

She couldn't stand to be in the car any longer. As soon as her mom put the car in park, Reagan flung her door open and hurried upstairs. Her mom said something, but Reagan couldn't hear and didn't care to ask. She ran up the stairs, flinging herself onto her bed, her head buried into her pillow.

She heard a light knock on the door, heard the door crack open.

"Reagan," her mom said, gently.

Reagan didn't reply, and her mom took her silence as an invitation to enter.

She sat on the edge of the bed, patting Reagan's leg.

"I know how that must feel," she said softly.

Reagan's eyes stung. How could her mom know how she was feeling? How Cora's life was coming together, taking shape while her own life was crumbling right in front of her eyes.

Reagan nodded, a small acknowledgement.

"But think of how all these years of you and Max excelling at almost everything you do felt to Cora. It's time she has her own thing," her mom said. She patted Reagan's leg again and stood, stooping down to kiss Reagan's cheek. "Won't you come join us downstairs?"

She shook her head. She couldn't stand to be down there.

"I'll come back up in a little bit," her mom said, kissing her on the head.

Reagan heard the door click shut, and then she was completely alone.

Chapter 46

THE ENERGY AROUND THE table was exuberant, and Cora's cheeks hurt from the smile plastered on her face. Her dad had come home from work early, surprising them when they got home. He wrapped her in a big hug and lifted her off the ground.

She devoured her dinner, and blushed when her dad asked, for the second time, to retell what Coach Parrish said. She reveled in the light-heartedness of their dinner.

But there was something in the back of her mind, nagging. Catching on her happiness and snagging like a pulled thread. In the middle of a laugh, she found herself caught on whatever it was holding her back. Deep within the well of her subconscious, something gnawed at her, and she couldn't shake the feeling. It was like when you were about to say something, and the sentence just floated off your tongue before you could give it words.

"Should we do a family movie night or something?" her mom asked. "Maybe Reagan will join us."

"Want me to go ask?" Cora volunteered.

Julie's eyes widened for a fleeting moment. "Sure, that would be great. Thanks, honey."

Cora climbed the stairs, listening through Reagan's door for any sound. It was quiet, and Cora wondered if Reagan was asleep. She knocked quietly on the door and waited for a response.

"What?" Reagan mumbled.

Cora opened the door and ventured inside. It was dark, eerily so, and the air was stale.

"Reagan? We're doing a family movie night tonight. Do you want to come downstairs?"

"I literally would rather do anything than that," Reagan said, her voice muffled.

"Okay," Cora said, retreating. "If you change your mind, we'll be downstairs."

Reagan didn't respond, just kept her head buried into her pillow.

Cora turned to head downstairs, but something pulled her to her room. She lifted the lid of the trinket box and checked on the compass. Still there. She breathed a sigh of relief. She had to visit Max tonight. She had to tell him the good news. How she found her second of bravery and how it set in motion a whole afternoon of amazing things.

She marched downstairs and joined her mom and dad for the movie.

For a fleeting moment, a pang of regret pricked Reagan's heart. She shouldn't be so cold to Cora, but she couldn't help herself. On the other hand, she didn't want those to be her last words to Cora. Maybe she would leave her a note, tucked away in her journal for her to find one day.

I'm sorry, she would say. *I wasn't myself. Congratulations on making the volleyball team.*

Reagan was slipping deeper and deeper into the chasm, and the energy to pull herself out was simply not there.

She remembered the compass, remembered how there was one place she had wanted to look before she was interrupted. She waited until she heard the rumble of the movie on the television downstairs before she snuck out of her room and into Cora's. She flicked on the light and moved straight for the trinket box. She lifted the lid and gasped when she saw what was inside.

Nestled inside, on a cheap elastic cord, was the compass, glittering in the light.

Reagan shook her head in disbelief. How had Cora gotten it? She changed her mind about writing Cora the note. No, Cora deserved those mean-spirited words. She had thieved this compass from Max, from their mom, and of all people in their family, she was the last to deserve it.

Reagan tucked the talisman into her palm and stalked back to her room. She pressed the golden globe so hard into her hand, the metal grooves pierced the skin of her palms.

In her room, Reagan flipped her light switch and closed the door. She tucked her legs underneath her and held the compass between her fingers, examining it closely. Max had carried this thing every day, and Reagan never understood why. Looking at it now, she still didn't understand. A chunk of gold with some embossing. Reagan wasn't even sure it worked properly. She flipped it over in her hand, absorbing all the intricate details, then closed her palm over it, holding it tightly in her hand. She stopped, hoping that some of Max's goodness would wear off onto her. She laid down, still clasping the compass. She took deep breaths.

Now that she'd found the compass, she could finally let go of the greased pipe she had been clinging to. Her grip strength was waning, and she was exhausted—physically, mentally, and emotionally. She had nothing left, nothing but the compass. She closed her eyes, letting her thoughts wander to the dark crevices of her mind.

Chapter 47

CORA REACHED THE TOP of the stairs and paused
outside of Reagan's room, listening intently. The nagging,
gnawing feeling hung over her, but she hadn't been able to
figure out exactly what it was yet. She would ask Max
when she saw him tonight.

She brushed her teeth quickly and changed into her
pajamas. Once in her room, she took out her sketchpad,
anxious to get sketching. She looked at the winter
wonderland scene in front of her. There was a soft knock
on the door.

"Yeah?" Cora asked.

Her mom cracked the door open and poked her head in.

"Just wanted to come say good night," she said,
stepping inside the room. Her dad followed.

"We're so proud of you," her dad said. Then quickly
added, "We would have been proud either way, but this is
extra exciting." He wrapped her in a giant hug.

"Really, sweetie. We are very excited for this new adventure." Her mom kissed her on the top of her head.

"Thanks," Cora said.

Her dad noticed the sketchpad on her desk. "Don't stay up too late," he said with a wink.

"Night, dear. We love you." Her mom gave her a final parting hug, and then they were gone.

As soon as the door clicked shut, Cora reached for the blue trinket box on her desk. When she lifted the lid, she gasped in astonishment.

The box was empty.

Okay, think Cora, she told herself. *Where else could you have put it? Nowhere, I know I put it in the trinket box. That's where I always put it. But it's not there, and no one else knows about it. But that is where I put it.* Cora had an intense internal dialogue, trying to think of where the compass could have gone. The bed? She pulled all the covers back, frantically searching for the little gold compass. It wasn't on her bed. She shook the comforter out, hoping it would fall from the folds. Nothing. She grabbed her pajamas from the night before and searched each pocket. It was nowhere to be found. Since no one knew she had the compass, since she technically maybe shouldn't even have the compass, she couldn't ask for help, or ask anyone if they had seen it.

Cora sank onto her bed, defeated and fighting back tears. The compass had been her lifeline to Max, and now without it, she was deserted and alone.

Cora laid back, her gaze floating up to the woven hanging above her. The crystals! The compass and the wall hanging were both souvenirs from the same trip. She wondered if the crystals were as charmed as the compass. She removed it from the hook on her wall and carried it over to her desk. Her gaze settled on the blue apatite. She plucked the blue-green stone from the woven web and clenched her fist around it. Then, she grabbed her sketchpad and pencil and started sketching. She drew the winter scene in front of her, taking time to ensure each feature was accurate. When her eyelids felt heavy, she let them fall.

Chapter 48

SOMETHING WAS OFF. CORA knew before she opened her eyes that something was different. The places she had accessed in the past always had an inexplicable light to them, a feeling of hope. But now, she shivered as feelings of despair and desperation cloaked her. This realm was darker, more sinister, devoid of any light.

A dark, dense fog settled around her, making it impossible to see. Frigid wind whipped about, carrying her red hair wildly in the air. The impenetrable fog and the fierce wind seemed to fight Cora's every step.

Cora knew Reagan was here. She knew this was the culmination of all of her journeys. Reagan. Cora recalled her conversation with Max when he'd told her that Reagan needed help, and somehow, on some subconscious level, Cora knew this was the moment for which she had been prepared.

To find Reagan, she had to get moving, but she didn't know where to go. She paced in circles, doubt increasing with each step.

The longer you wait, the bigger it gets. Move. Sometimes the only way forward is to do the next best thing. The next best thing was to take a step, any step. She listened intently, straining to hear anything amidst the haze surrounding her.

She followed her instincts and started walking, feeling more confident now that she had a purpose. Even though she couldn't see her feet through the thick mist, she felt as if she were being guided.

Walk through your fear, she reminded herself with each step. *What's on the other side of your fear?* She couldn't see far ahead and was taking steps of blind faith. *Sometimes you have to step into the darkness to see the light.* She was taking many, many steps in the darkness and had yet to see the light.

There was something eerie about this realm, a darkness that Cora couldn't recognize. She couldn't shake the feeling that someone, something, was watching her, and Cora found herself looking over her shoulder to ensure she wasn't being followed.

Cora heard a guttural cry from somewhere ahead, and instinctively called out.

"Reagan?"

There was silence as her voice echoed off the absent walls.

Finally, after the silence, a small voice replied.

"What are you doing here?"

"Where are you?" Cora ignored her question, listening to the sound of Reagan's voice and trying to find her. The swirling mist made visibility nearly impossible, and Cora was relying on little more than her own intuition to get to Reagan.

"It doesn't matter, Cora," Reagan said, and started to cry. "Please just go away." Her voice was getting louder, but Cora wondered if that was the wind, playing tricks on her ears.

"I can't, Reagan. I won't." Cora called out. "How did you get here?"

She already knew the answer, but if she could get Reagan talking about the compass, maybe she could find her quicker.

Reagan was silent and Cora worried her diversion tactic had backfired.

"I don't actually know," Reagan finally replied. Her voice was so close, Cora knew she was only a few steps ahead. Cora walked forward in the heavy fog.

"Reagan?" She said softly.

"How did you find me?" Reagan asked.

Cora bent and the sisters were face to face. Reagan sat hunched against what looked like a giant boulder.

"Cora, what is this place?" she asked. Her bottom lip quivered, and tears spilled from her eyelids. "I don't know what is happening."

Cora looked around, unsure of how to answer. She didn't know what this place was, but she knew they needed to get out of here quickly. The ominous feeling around her seeped into her skin.

"Do you have Max's compass with you?" Cora asked.

Reagan extended her hand and opened it, exposing the gold ball. Even in the darkness, it seemed to glimmer.

"Okay, good." Cora said matter-of-factly. "Don't let that go. Whatever you do, don't let go of that compass."

Reagan nodded.

"But... Where are we?" Reagan asked.

"I don't know how it all works exactly, but the compass is a sort of portal," Cora explained. "And it can transport you to wherever you're at in your mind." Cora looked around, worried that Reagan's mind was filled with such darkness.

Reagan looked at her in disbelief.

"I know, it doesn't make a lot of sense, but I promise it's real," Cora said. She looked around again. "And Reagan, based on where we are, and based on some other things, I know you—we—aren't in a good place."

Cora looked at her sister and her heart filled with compassion. A love she had never felt for Reagan before swelled within her.

Reagan shook her head.

"Cora, I'm a mess," she said through tears.

"It's okay to be a mess," Cora said, stroking Reagan's hair away from her eyes. "It's just not okay to stay there for too long."

"I don't know how to be anything other than a mess right now," Reagan admitted, tears streaming down her face.

"It's hard to see when everything around you feels broken. But I promise there is a world worth living in."

"That's easy for you to say, Cora," Reagan said skeptically. "I just don't see how I can dig myself out of this hole. It's so deep and feels like every time I try to take a step out, the ground beneath me gives way and I'm right back where I started. And the thought of doing it all is just too much. It's too hard."

"Reagan," Cora said bluntly. "There is one way out of here. You need to dig down deep inside yourself and see what you're going to fight for."

Cora looked at Reagan, trying to see into her soul, to discern what she was willing to do.

Reagan nodded. "I don't want to die, Cora," she said softly. "I don't want to. It just sometimes seems like the only way out. Sometimes I don't see a way out."

"Focus on taking the next best step," Cora said. "One single step. Can you manage to stand?"

"I think so," Reagan said, nodding and stood, her legs shaking, her knees nearly buckling.

"Okay, good," Cora encouraged her. "Now what?"

"I don't know, Cora," Reagan said, her eyes pleading.

"What is the next step, Reagan?" Cora asked.

"It all seems impossible." Reagan gazed around her, looking for the next step. She evaluated the giant boulder behind her. "Maybe this way?"

"Focus on the step ahead of you," Cora reminded her. She remembered how Max had coached her with these same phrases. "You can climb mountains, Reagan. You choose to. You have to be brave and you have to want it."

Reagan nodded and Cora could tell she was summoning all the courage within her. One second of bravery. She watched Reagan in awe, watched the moment Reagan found her courage. She stepped confidently forward and took a step onto the boulder, lifting her body into the air. She moved with ease for a few steps, her confidence guiding her like a beacon.

"Reagan you're doing awesome," Cora called from below.

She didn't realize this would be a test of *her* physical fear as well. As she watched Reagan ascend, Cora's own fear intensified.

"The longer you wait, the bigger it gets," she said to herself, and sent a silent plea to Max, summoning her courage. She found it and acted immediately, placing her foot in a small crevice and stepping upward.

Reagan was ahead of her in the distance when she called out.

"Cora! It's really windy. I'm worried I'm going to fall!" The wind contorted her voice, and Cora couldn't tell where the sound was coming from.

"Keep going!" Cora encouraged her. "Just focus on the one step ahead of you!" She hoped the wind carried her message to her sister.

She told herself the same thing. *Keep going. Focus on the one step ahead of you.*

"Reagan!" Cora called to the wind. "Can you see the top?"

Don't you quit, Cora, a voice from within urged her. *You keep going. The fight is always worth fighting.*

"Cora!" Cora heard a shrill scream. Rocks scattered around her, and Cora had a sickening feeling that Reagan had fallen. Or jumped.

"Reagan!" She screamed into the wind.

"I slipped!" she screamed, terror rising in her voice. "I'm barely holding on!"

Cora moved forward, step after agonizing step until she found Reagan, holding tightly to the ledge by her fingertips.

Cora steeled herself as much as possible and grabbed Reagan's wrist.

"Reagan," she said quickly, infusing her voice with as much authority as she could muster. "You need to climb back up. You've got to get your feet on sure footing."

Reagan nodded, but Cora could see doubt settling in Reagan's eyes.

"But Cora, just in case something happens--"

Cora cut her off.

"Don't you dare quit, Reagan," she said brusquely. "You keep holding on, you keep going. The fight is always fighting. You didn't come this far to stop now. You came this far because you're going to conquer this mountain. And you're going to conquer your fear, your doubt, all the things. You're going to do that because you're Reagan, and you're the toughest girl I know!"

Cora's vigor kindled a spark in Reagan, and Cora saw the fire ignite in her eyes. Using all of her strength, Reagan pulled herself back up, Cora steadying her. When she made it back up to secure ground, she collapsed into an exhausted heap.

"Thank you, Cora," Reagan said, breathlessly. "You have no idea how you've saved me."

Reagan looked deeply into Cora's eyes, and Cora thought she knew more than she would like to know about how close she had been to losing Reagan.

"Let's get to the top of this thing and get out of here," Cora said. The mist below them had turned a darker shade of grey, and Cora worried how dark this place could get before it consumed them.

They went to the summit, side by side, and sat together at the peak. Cora leaned into Reagan, catching her breath.

Cora looped her arm through Reagan's. She looked around again, unable to shake the feeling that someone, something, else was there, watching. It was then she saw it, the faint green-yellow glow emanating from the rising fog. She narrowed her eyes. All along she thought that light was a beacon from Max, but he didn't know anything about it. Now the light had an eerie glow. If it wasn't Max, who, or what, was calling to her? She turned her attention to Reagan. She wanted to get out of there.

"Still have that compass?" Cora asked.

Reagan nodded and extended her hand once again. She opened it, revealing the compass.

"Make a fist around it," she instructed Reagan. She closed her hand around Reagan's, and squeezed her eyes shut.

Chapter 49

"CORA?" HER MOM CALLED her from downstairs. "Mia is here, sweetie!"

Cora slipped on her pink high-top sneakers and bounded down the stairs, not even slowing down when she passed Reagan's room. As she came down the stairs, she saw Reagan sitting at the kitchen table. Reagan looked up from her homework and smiled.

"Hey, Mia!" Cora called, seeing her friend at the counter. "You ready?"

"If you are," Mia said, smiling. She held her bike helmet in her hand.

"Cora, not too long, okay? Dad and I are facilitating that support group tonight and need to leave in about an hour." Julie glanced at the clock and looked back at Cora. "And Reagan has a soccer game after that, if you two want to join us."

"Okay, Mom," Cora agreed, nodding. She looked at Reagan seated at the kitchen table, hunched over a psychology assignment. She was studying to be a psychologist at a community college, and Cora knew she would make an awesome therapist one day. "Soccer game sounds fun."

Cora pulled on a hoodie, the front emblazoned with a fiery volleyball soaring through the air and her last name and volleyball number, 21, across the back.

The compass sat in the blue trinket box in Cora's room. She hadn't used it since that dark day with Reagan, but she wasn't quite ready to part with it yet. Besides, she had a nagging feeling that someone had been watching her in that last visit, a feeling she hadn't been able to shake.

Better keep the compass, just in case, she thought to herself.

Cora and Mia opened the door and hopped on their bikes.

"Where to?" Cora asked.

Mia was already pedaling ahead of Cora. "Follow me!" she shouted over her shoulder.

Cora pedaled hastily after Mia, ascending a steep hill. Her tousled red hair blew in every direction around her. She stood and pumped her legs harder, straining to catch up with Mia. She climbed the hill, higher and higher, rising like the Phoenix she was. As she peaked the hill, she paused at the top, taking in everything around her.

Cora couldn't help but think she really was living an epic life.

About the Author

Courtney Daybell has lived most of her life in the mountains of Utah, with a brief stint under the big city lights of Manhattan, New York, where she worked for a local magazine. When she isn't writing, Courtney can be found spending time with her husband and three children, listening to true crime podcasts, or on the eternal quest for the perfect chocolate chip cookie recipe.

From the Ash She Rises is her first novel. For more information, visit her website at courtneydaybell.com, or email hello@courtneydaybell.com.